It Came to Pass

A Timeless Christian Love Story

JOHN MARINELLI

Preface

"It Came To Pass" is a timeless love story, all centered on the love and protection of God.

The book tells the story of romance, war and tragedy that flows through WWII and the Vietnam conflict. The storyline will follow Bill and Sarah, childhood sweethearts and how they demonstrate faith in troubled times.

Central to the story is a golden coin that was lost for over 300 years, found by an American soldier in France during WW II and lost again by a ten-year old boy in a little town north of Odessa, TX.

The story will also address some modern day social issues and will touch on God's Will, Man's Destiny, Faith, Loyalty, Free Will and The Authority of The Bible.

This is a fictional story, however the WW II and Vietnam facts are true and are based upon public records.

The reader will experience the invasion of Normandy, the tragedy of war, what it feels like to not know who you really are, and the joy of seeing the hand of God restoring life and love lost but not forgotten. He or she will ride overland on a public bus with other folks on their way to an encounter with a "Mysterious Stranger" of Supernatural origin.

The reader will also be included in interviews with those that met the Mysterious Stranger.

Introduction

There is a favorite sentence in the bible that helps me to move along in life with a positive perspective. The phrase is, "It Came To Pass." God showed me this many years ago. He said to me, "Many things will enter your reality. Some will be good and some not so good but rest assured that they will come but not stay. The will pass through your life leaving behind sorrow or blessings. They come only to pass away in to oblivion. Only My word will stay and accomplish what I desire for you.

With this truth in mind, I set out to create a story that reveals situations and events that come to pass and the hand of God in the lives of those that are suffering under it's wake of destruction.

Our story begins in the summer of 1993 at the home of Joe Jenkins. It's Joe's 68th birthday celebration. Joe was a WWII survivor of the battle of Normandy. The war *came to pass* leaving him wounded along with many other army veterans. He was somewhat shell shocked. He spent many months in recovery, went on to college and became a successful Dentist.

Joe fell in love with Mary Blessidt, a girl from California, while attending a dental convention. They married and now enjoy life in north central Florida on a 10-acre hobby farm. Their only son, Mark, is visiting with his two children, Sandy, age 15 and Johnny, age 16. Mark is a widower trying to raise his two children after their mother died of lung cancer.

As the family all sat down on the "Wrap-A-Round" porch, Johnny asked his grandpa to tell some war stories. He wanted to know what it was really like because he was all into the old WWII movies.

Joe was reluctant to talk about those days because of the trauma and horrible scenes of dying men that still haunted him when he slept. However, he agreed when the rest of the family also encouraged him to talk about D-Day.

What will transpire are the words and thoughts of Joe Jenkins. This is how he remembers it, in his own words.

A Portrait of The Past

OK folks, I'll do the best I can to remember the events leading up to and during the invasion of Normandy. However, it's been 50 years. I have never told anyone about what happened to me back then, not even my wife or only son.

It all began with Bill Anderson and Sarah Johnson, my very best friends. It was 1943 and the United States was up to its elbows in WW II. By November, gasoline, bicycles, footwear, silk, nylon, fuel oil, stoves, meat, lard, shortening, margarine, processed foods, dried fruits, canned milk, firewood and coal, jams, jellies and butter would all be rationed. The United States was at war with Japan, Germany and other Nazi led forces.

Women went to work to fill the vacancies of men that went to war. Many factories stopped making consumer goods and retooled for the production of tanks, airplanes, guns and ammunition.

Young men were joining the military as volunteers. Bill Anderson, my best friend and I were no exception. We were typical of 1943 American youth. We were patriotic and ready and willing to defend our nation from the tyranny of Nazism. We would never ever think of burning the national flag like some young people do today. We had respect for the flag and the country it represented.

Bill and I were "Allstars" at Midland High School. We both lettered in basketball and played in every game. It was our senior year. We did everything together from homework to taking girls to the school dances on Saturday nights. We planned to join the army after graduation and do our part to defend our country.

Bill was head over heals in love with a gal named Sarah Johnson. She was a cheerleader at Midland High. They had several classes together and Bill walked her to class and carried her books as boyfriends were expected to do in those days. They were secretly engaged with plans to marry after finishing high school. They had been childhood sweethearts since the 6th grade. As I recall, Sarah was obsessed with marriage, children, and being a good wife.

It was hard for us to imagine being combat ready soldiers. We never even got in a fight after school. I guess you would say that we were popular and liked by everyone. Armed conflict and killing was not in our vocabulary.

However, we both felt deeply about protecting our country and way of life. The thinking back in 1943 was, "If we don't fight, who will?"

We all worked side by side for the war effort by participating in scrap metal drives, local military family support visits, and even letter writing to lonely soldiers.

Sarah was afraid for Bill. She often was overwhelmed by thoughts that he would go off to war and not come home. The thought of Bill dying on a foreign battlefield was terrifying. She never let Bill know her deepest fears but I knew because she would share them with me. She felt that he had enough to think about without taking on her problems.

Bill always wanted to get married and settle down but I was a ladies' man. I dated a lot in high school and often went on double dates with Bill and Sarah. Those days were the best times of my life.

High School Sweethearts

Sandy jumped in to interrupt grandpa Joe's thoughts. She said, "Tell us more about Sarah & Bill." Ok, said grandpa Joe. Where do I begin? Oh yea, I remember. Sarah and Bill were both Christians. They attended church and were part of the youth group. Sarah was a lot stronger in her faith than Bill.

I remember a time when Bill told me about skipping lunch so he and Sarah could smooch. Johnny and Sandy began to giggle but grandpa Joe just continued on.

It was on a Friday. No, It was Thursday. What difference does a day make? It was during the senior lunch period at Midland High. Sarah and Bill skipped out and snuck off by themselves for one more of those secret rendezvous. Bill began flirting with Sarah as he always did and telling her how much he loved her. They kissed and kissed and Bill started to move beyond the flirting stage but Sarah was reluctant.

Sarah pushed Bill away saying, "Not until we are married." "You know how I feel about that." "We are Christians, remember?"

Bill was frustrated and said "But I am going off to war and may never come back. Don't you think we should, well, you know…. It's only a few weeks before we will be married"

Sarah couldn't help thinking about the youth pastor's message that previous Sunday. It was on pre-marital sex and what the Bible said. She just blurted out, "The Bible says we would be fornicators and those folks do not get into heaven."

Bill started to get angry saying," Who are they to tell us what we can or cannot do"

Sarah came back with a definition for "They". She looked into Bill's eyes and said, "Have you ever heard of, "**The Father**" "**The Son**" and "**The Holy Ghost**"? That's who they are. Now let's go back to class."

Bill told me afterwards that he felt that Sarah was using the Bible and God as a crutch so she wouldn't have to be sexually involved with him. He began to have serious reservations about Sarah but those feeling just dropped away when Sarah told him the next day that she loved him and if he really loved her, they could exercise some restraint and be a blessing to God. She said, "We respect the laws of our country. Shouldn't we also respect the laws of God?"

So Bill and Sarah pledged themselves to each other and to being honorable Christians. They wanted God in their married life and wanted to know His will.

Sometimes, when the three of us were together, we would make sport of God's will, just to have fun and laugh. Bill jokingly would say, "Maybe God wants us to fly to the moon in a space ship or maybe He will use us to change the toilet paper in the school bathrooms."

Sarah would laugh and then she would get serious saying, "Maybe God has great things in store for us. All we have to do is to continue in what we know is truly His will and we will walk right into our destiny."

Destiny would soon knock on their door and mine. God's will was about to collide head on with WW II.

Bill and Sarah had a standing Friday night date but not until the basketball game was over. Sarah had duties as a cheerleader and Bill played forward guard for the Midland High Golden Tornadoes. I played center.

The team was in 1st place among all AAA statewide high schools. We were about a week away from the semi-finals that would determine which teams would face off for the state championship.

I remember a time when Bill and I were practicing our

"Free-Throw" shots and talking about the semi-finals. I said, "Bill? What if we loose this game? We'll be shut out of the tournament."

Bill stopped shooting the ball and said, "That's why we are not going to fail. We have come this far and we will win. It's up to you and me buddy, so hang in there and be tough." That's the type of guy he was, always optimistic.

Sarah was passing by, going to the girl's locker room and overheard some of our conversation and what Bill said to me. She jumped into the middle of our conversation and, grabbed Bill's hands and said, "I love you and love conquers all" Then she looked over at me and said, "Repeat after me…Winner's don't quit and quitters don't see themselves as winners."

Then she said, " We are winners and I can see us holding that trophy as the crowd goes wild. See it with me and then go out there and make it happen." I guess that's why she was a cheerleader…always cheering us on.

Sure enough, Bill and I, supported by the rest of the team, won the game by twelve points and went on to become the 1943 State Basketball Champs. Later at the victory dance, Sarah had to rub it in and said to both of us, "I told you so. We are winners. We are champions"

Later that week, after all the excitement of winning the state championship, Bill told me that he and Sarah sat down with both parents and seriously talked about their marriage and plans for the future.

Sarah was like most other girls growing up in the 40s. She wanted to stay home, have babies and be a good supportive wife to Bill, just like her mother was to her dad. She even told her mother that she was almost 18, the same age that her mom was when she married. Then she told me that she looked over at her dad and said, "If 18 was grown up enough for you and mom, it is for me too." Well needless to say, her dad was a bit upset.

According to Bill, Sarah's dad spoke up saying, "That's right but we were more mature and I went on to college while your mother stayed with her parents until my graduation. We started married life with me having a good job, not running off to war. You'll be stranded and alone in a strange army town." I guess Sarah's dad was just being protective of his oldest daughter.

Then, according to Sarah, her mother spoke up in her defense saying, "She's right, we did the same thing and it worked out for us. I guess it's ok, as long as we can support you and you stay here until Bill gets settled."

So Sarah looked at Bill and said, "What do you think?" He replied, "That's ok with me." The next week Sarah and her mother begin the invitation list for Sarah's wedding. Meanwhile Bill and I made our own plans to join the army.

The Secret Enlistment

You're probably bored by now with my rambling. Maybe I need to stop. "Don't stop grandpa", said Johnny. "This is like watching a movie. What happened next?"

Well then, said grandpa Joe. Where was I? Oh yeah. Bill and I met up that same afternoon to discuss our new adventure into "Army Life." We didn't want to be drafted. We talked a lot about being soldiers. It was like being a grown up because we would be out on our own and in the uniform of our country. It all sounded real good. We never though once about getting killed or even wounded. That stuff always happened to the other guy, which we didn't know personally.

Bill remembered what the army recruiter said about enlisting and being drafted. On September 16, 1940, the United States instituted the Selective Training and Service Act, which required all men between the ages of 21 - 45 to register for the draft. This was the first peacetime draft in United States' history.

During WW II, the army accepted recruits at 16 but those soldiers could not be deployed to the front lines until age 18. We knew that we needed to wait until our 18th birthday to enlist so we could go to the front lines and fight. But that was only a few weeks away.

We planned to enlist under the "buddy" system. I pushed Bill to join up while we were still in school. I said, why couldn't we go right away? If we did, it would keep my dad from hounding me about college. I didn't want to go to college right out of high school. It would be as if I were hiding from my responsibility to defend our flag and great country. I was proud of being an American and wanted to invest my time as a soldier to insure that we would still be free.

Freedom was important to all of us. We knew that those that came before us paid for our freedom with the blood of their sons and family members. It wasn't like today. No one burned the flag or even thought of badmouthing our country. We were proud of our heritage and were willing to die if necessary so our families can live in freedom.

There was too much at stake to sit in a college learning about Plato and ancient history. The war was far more interesting. After all, Bill and I played Cowboys and Indians and even WAR with our friends when we were little. It all seemed like another game to play but this time as grown ups.

The "Buddy System" was a special program where two friends could join at the same time and be guaranteed of staying together throughout their enlistments. They would go to boot camp together and be assigned to the same military base when training was over.

Well, I kept on Bill until he said, "Ok, we can join now but delay our departure until after my wedding. But don't tell Sarah. I will do that later. Sarah and I are going to be married right out of high school. Then we're going on a honeymoon. Then we will leave for Boot Camp."

That same week Bill and I went to the army recruiting office to talk to the recruiter. I never knew there would be so much paperwork. We needed to get a transcript of our grades, a letter from our parents, and take a lot of tests. My dad was reluctant to give me a letter but finally gave in to my plea.

The army wanted to know if we were smart or not. They tested us for being crazy, stupid, quick-tempered and a bunch of other things.

Well, we passed with flying colors. Bill did a little better than I did but we both made it. They even did background checks on us to see if we had any criminal records. If we did, they would have rejected us right then and there. They also did an FBI investigation into our habits and loyalties to see if we were ever involved with communism, secret societies or collaboration with the "Third Reich." That is what we called Nazism.

I guess the army wanted to be sure that we were loyal Americans and willing to fight for "Old Glory." Just so you all know, "Old Glory" is a reference to the Flag. Men have fought in wars since the 1700 under its banner, defending their right to be free and to govern themselves.

My Old Girlfriend, Susie

Grandpa Joe's wife, Mary, began to laugh and Joe did too. He said, "I know why you are laughing. It's because you want me to tell them about Suzie, right? She said, "Yep, go ahead. It will be fun to hear it from your lips."

Ok, but I will go on record as an innocent bystander, even though she was my X-Girlfriend. You see, Suzie and I dated for about six months. I even asked her to go steady but she refused saying that she wanted the freedom to date other guys. She had a way about her when she batted her eyes and walked down the halls of our school. It would drive the boys crazy.

Well, enough of that. After sharing her with half the football team, I dropped her and went on to other high school beauties. After I dropped Suzie, she turned her eyes to Bill and didn't care at all about Sarah's claim on him.

Bill and Sarah were sweethearts and back then it meant an exclusive relationship. However, their trust in each other

fell on shaky ground when Suzie, Bill's new lab partner, started to bat her eyes at Bill every day in chemistry class. It was hard for Bill to not flirt back or act as though nothing was going on. He liked Suzie and there was definite chemistry between them.

He often spoke of Suzie and asked me lots of questions like, "Is she easy?" I told him that he better run for the hills because Suzie could and would destroy him. But Bill found flirting to be fun and made it his classroom past time.

One day in chemistry class Suzie looked into Bill's eyes and said, "We should get together outside of school and have some fun. My parents will be away this weekend and we could, well you know, be alone." She then took his hand and said, "What do you think?"

I laughed as Bill was telling me the details. I told him that Suzie was a snake and he should watch out. Bill, like any red blooded American male, was overjoyed and felt a rush of power. He could be, "The Man", "The King of The Hill", or just "Another Fool." It was all up to him and hung on his answer to Suzie's sexual invitation.

I can still remember, after more than 50 years, how Bill felt inside. You should have seen him when he was telling me. He was sweating, anxious and even trembling a little because he knew that Sarah would break off their engagement if she found out.

Bill's jubilation quickly turned into betrayal and inward

shame. He struggled within himself with being loyal to Sarah and enjoying selfish sexual pleasures with Suzie. A storm raged in his mind raining down feelings of desire for Suzie and shame that he would even think that way.

The though that no one would find out kept coming into his mind, saying, "It's ok to be with Suzie." But somehow that thought just didn't settle in his spirit. He began to reason that even if he got away with it, he would still be a fool because it was against the will of God. It was then that he knew God was talking to him.

Suzie said it again in other words, "What's a matter Bill? Don't you want to be with me? Sarah will never find out, I promise."

Bill said that he withdrew his hand from Suzie' and said, "Even if Sarah never found out, it would still be wrong and I do not want to live my life with Sarah in betrayal of her trust. She is worthy of my loyalty, even when my desires turn to you." The battle of the mind was just as strong as the battle overseas but Bill stayed true to Sarah's love.

We all knew Suzie was angry that Bill refused to be with her. She told Bill that she had gone to so much trouble planning every detail in her mind of how they would raid her dad's liquor cabinet and what music they would play to set the mood. She had it all figured out and was not expecting a rejection.

"Why can't you play along," she said. We could have so

much fun being together. But Bill just kept saying, "No, It's not right" Then Suzie began to scold Bill saying, "You're not a man. You're just a little boy. I guess I am just too much for you"

Bill replied, "Don't be mad. You are a really good looking gal but I gave my heart away a long time ago to Sarah."

Suzie began to cry saying, "We'll see about that. I am going to tell Sarah of all about the lab flirtations and how you kept coming on to me and wanting me. You'll be the laughing stock of the entire school. Why don't you just be with me and get it over with? You know you want to"

According to Bill, He responded to Suzie's threat by saying, "Sure I flirted with you in chemistry class but I never thought it would go this far. I thought it was just a game. I didn't mean to hurt you. I thought you understood that it was just a game" Then Suzie lashed out at Bill saying, "well I didn't understand." "What you were thinking was wrong. I am going to hurt you like you hurt me. When I am through, Sarah will reject you like you rejected me."

Bill said he watched Suzie walk away in tears and wonders what he could do to fix the mess he was in.

Bill did the only thing any honest Christian would do in the same situation. He confessed everything to Sarah but mixed the truth with a few white lies. He said, "Sarah? I have something I need to tell you. You know that I have chemistry lab with Suzie. She has been my lab partner all year. Well, she wanted me to spend the weekend with her and I refused. She got real mad and said she was going to tell you a bunch of lies so you would break up with me."

Sarah replied, "You mean those lies about you flirting with her all year and the suggestive remarks about fooling around?"

Bill stammered a bit and said, "She's already talked with you, huh? But let me explain, it was just a game that she started and I played along because she was my lab partner. I didn't mean anything by it"

Sarah said, "Likely story!" "Let me be absolutely clear. You are my guy and I am worthy of your respect and loyalty. If you are going to be a flirt and dance around with every girl that looks at you, I am not your gal. You can take a hike right now."

So Bill promised to not be a "Skirt Chaser" and to never again flirt with another girl. Bill was forgiven and he and Sarah were once again sweethearts. All was well except for Bill's secret decision to join the army and leave right after Bill and Sarah's honeymoon. She didn't know and he was afraid to tell her.

Now a few days later I ran into Bill on the way to school and told him of my problem. I was always getting into some situation that had to do with girls and I often went to Bill for advice. He had a cool head and didn't mind listening.

So I said, "I met this girl that just transferred into Midland

High. She and I got along really great but she dropped a bombshell on me just as we were ending our first date. Guess what she told me?"

Bill replied, "She probably said she was really a boy or something. That stuff is popping up in high schools all around the country these days."

I said, "No, she is not that way. It's worse. She likes guys and girls and one day wants to have a marriage of three, not two. She wants to know if that's ok with me"

Bill wanted to know what I told her. He said, "Well, what did you tell her?"

"I said that I'd get back to her. What do you think, Bill?"

Bill laughed and said, "After the stern lecture by Sarah about being exclusive to her, I'd tell her to take a hike. Why are you thinking of being with two girls when you can't hardly manage one? Besides, God frowns on such behavior. It is un-natural and against His desire for man."

I spoke up and said, " Who says it's wrong, God? How can I know for sure?"

Bill cleared his throat and slowly spoke, " Sarah showed me in the Bible where it says God made man in His own image and likeness and that He made them male and fe-male, not male and two females or two girls or two boys. Sarah says this is what makes each of us special and of value."

So I accepted Sarah's Biblical answer, explained to me by Bill and we shifted gears and looked towards Bill's wedding and going into the army.

"Pot Luck" & "Finger Pointing"

Graduation finally arrived and Bill and Sarah, with their parent's approval, married and began preparations to set up housekeeping in Sarah's parent's basement apartment. It was small but adequate and was all theirs to start off a new life together. There was still that question of joining the army. For now, it was just fun to be together and be grown up.

The Midland Community Church youth pastor married Bill and Sarah in their church. They spent the rest of the afternoon at the wedding reception, which was held in the church's fellowship hall.

Bill and Sarah could not afford an expensive fancy wedding but the church family blessed them with gifts, money and lots of food for the reception. They had a guest list of 40 friends, relatives and their church family.

Everyone brought a dish to pass and drinks to share. It was great. Folks cane with platters of meats, bakery items, several cases of soda pop, salads and even home made ice cream. It was one big, "Pot Luck Wedding," for sure.

The bridal party was made up of three bridesmaids and three ushers. Sarah's little sister Ann was the flower girl. I

was the "Best Man" and Marcie, Sarah's best friend, was the "Maid of Honor."

Bill and Sarah danced the night away with their closest friends until Suzie crashed the party claiming she was pregnant and Bill was the father.

Suzie started sobbing and said, "He is the father of my unborn baby." Bill's dad ushered the girl to a back room and calmed her down. Bill's mother drilled her to learn all the details so her story could be verified.

I couldn't help but laugh at the whole thing because I know it was all "Finger Pointing" lies designed to hurt Bill. However, Bill was still on trial in the court of public opinion. Fortunately, Suzie's display of anger got no sympathy from the wedding guests. They all knew what type of girl she was. Her story just didn't jive. Finally the parents of the bride asked her to leave or be arrested. So Suzie left but not before cursing Bill and his entire wedding guests.

Now Sarah was not so sure that Suzie was lying. She took Bill off to one side and asked the big question. "Did you sleep with Suzie and is she really pregnant? You better tell me the truth because if I find out later, I'll never forgive you."

Bill told Sarah the truth, "It is not true, none of it. She is upset because I rejected her and told her in no uncertain terms that you were and still are my heartthrob."

Johnny interrupted and said, "What did Sarah say" I told Johnny to hold on, I'll get to it. Then I drank some of my Ice Tea, stretched my legs and said, here's what Sarah said, "OK but remember, I'll never forgive you if you are lying."

So the wedding day continued and everyone celebrated Bill and Sarah's new life together. That eventful night ended with Bill and Sarah spending their first night together as husband and wife in their new basement apartment. Bill said, "The best part of the night was when he heard Sarah softly say, "Come to bed my love."

Where's Mary? She wanted to know if we were done? I told her that we had just begun. I like happy endings but there is a lot more to Bill and Sarah's story.

High School sweethearts turned into lovers and lovers go on honeymoons. Bill and Sarah's honeymoon was a gift from Bill's dad; an all expense paid one-week stay at Niagara Falls, the most favored honeymoon spot among newlyweds of that day. It was perfect for the new couple to blend together and become one.

The next day Bill and Sarah flew out to Niagara Falls for a full week of fun and relaxation. It was their special time to be together.

Bill told me later that upon their arrival at the falls, the big welcome sign said: 3,160 tons of water flows over Niagara Falls every second. When he was reading the sign he heard

Sarah laughing and she said, "I guess we are in the right place."

During their honeymoon, Bill and Sarah talked about how life would be for them being in the middle of WW II and afterwards.

Bill and I both wanted to be realtors and work in new construction. We both felt that a lot of GI's would return from war wanting houses and starting families. It would be the perfect time to make a lot of money and raise a family of our own.

Sarah was glad that Bill was thinking ahead and wanted to provide for their new life together. She thought, "This will drive Bill to fight hard to stay safe and come back from the war alive."

She was glad that he hadn't signed up yet. She wanted as much time with her husband as possible. After all, one less soldier wouldn't make much difference. That's what Bill told me on the phone when I called his hotel room to check on things. He told me all about what they were up to and that he had not yet told Sarah about joining up.

The newlyweds ate in the local restaurants, shopped in the nearby stores and watched the water flow over the falls for hours at a time. Bill said that it was spectacular. Everything was perfect until Bill finally told Sarah that he and I had already joined up under the, "Buddy System." We were scheduled to leave for boot camp one week after their return to Midland.

After we left for boot camp I asked Bill how things went between them when he dropped the bomb of joining up right away on Sarah. He said that Sarah was furious and lashed out at him saying, "How could you do such a thing without discussing it with me? What if you never come back? What do I do then? You could have waited and been drafted or maybe the war would end sooner and you might not have gone at all. Now you have placed our marriage and future in jeopardy"

Bill said that he started laughing. He laughed it off saying, "They can't kill me. I just got married. I have to come back."

Bill said that they went back and forth with Sarah crying all the time and Bill saying it would be ok. They fell asleep in each other's arms to the sound of the water rushing over the falls. Sarah was forced to accept what was soon to be.

Sarah and Bill awoke to the reality that this new day was the last day of their honeymoon. Tomorrow, they would go home. Sarah looked at Bill and smiled, saying, "It's ok. We will work it out together. What will be will be. God will provide and take care of both of us."

Bill was glad that Sarah was no longer angry. He hugged her and said, "That's right, God will watch over us."

Bill said that they spent the day together and packed that night for an early departure. Bedtime came quickly with so much to do. However, Bill told me that he tossed and turned and was troubled in his spirit. He began to dream and saw himself and me in the thick of battle and watched, as if it were a movie, seeing himself being killed in action. He woke up screaming in a cold sweat. He said, "No, God no, I don't want to die"

Sarah woke up when Bill began to scream and tried to wake him up saying, "It's just a dream. You are having a nightmare. Wake up, Bill. Wake up!"

Bill finally woke up but was still trembling. He said, "It seemed so real, as if I were really there."

"So what happened?" Mark, Joe's son blurted out. "Did Bill back out of the enlistment? Did Bill get killed in action?"

Hold on folks. This is my story and what happened has to be explained properly.

That night Sarah comforted Bill and they cuddled and Bill fell asleep again. At least that's what Bill told me. He woke up at 6 a.m. still shaking inside. He didn't want to go to war anymore but had no honorable way out. He had to go. So Bill kept it all inside and never told Sarah the full dream. All she knew was that he had a nightmare that he couldn't remember.

However, Bill never forgot the dream. He felt like he had jumped into the future and saw his own death. It haunted him for weeks until he remembered the youth pastor's last message before he went on his honeymoon.

Bill quickly went back into his memory trying to recall

all of what his youth pastor said. All he could remember was something about God working everything together for good. He held on to that thought all through boot camp and our deployment.

Bill said that their last night together was spent talking, kissing and making love. Sarah wanted Bill to know that she loved him deeply and would be there for him when he returned. They prayed together as the sun rose over the falls bringing a new day.

Bill promised that he would see her again and they would pick up where they left off. A week later Bill's dad drove us to the bus station and we departed for boot camp.

Boot Camp And Deployment

Ten Hut! Get in line you maggots. God may have your soul but I've got everything else. If you are a sissy, go home. We make boys into men, fighting men that will protect our country.

Who Wants To Be A Man?

Boot camp was not what Bill and I had expected. We were athletic but boot camp was triple the exercise, plus lots of book study and attitude adjustments…much more than high school. I can remember Bill looking at me and saying, "They are trying to cram years of knowledge into ten weeks of training. How are we expected to remember it all?"

I laughed and replied, "We have to remember because if we don't, we will fail the final exam and stay in this hell hole another ten weeks."

So we studied hard and practice all the drills. I was honored as an expert marksman and Bill was promoted to company commander. I guess we both displayed leadership skills and as a result were selected for advanced training to become combat ready commandoes. We were being groomed to lead men into the largest armed invasion ever staged.

Basic Combat Training (BCT) is basic training or boot camp for civilians who want to join the military. It turns civilians into soldiers. We learned to march and shoot a riffle. They taught us survival skills and prepared us for life in the army. It was an intense 10 weeks.

Bill got a letter from Sarah almost every day but it was hard to write back because he was so tired after 12+ hours of drills, instruction and being yelled at by our drill sergeant. We told ourselves that we could do this and we did.

We finally finished BCT and went on for another 3-weeks of advanced combat training where we learned hand-to-hand combat, how to gather and use intelligence, war strategies and more survival skills.

Bill had an opportunity to call home and talk with Sarah. It was after midnight but that was ok with her. Bill wanted to hear her voice one more time before shipping out to Europe. We never did get a furlough after boot camp and advanced training school. So Bill called home and Sarah answered the phone at 12:17 A. M. and she immediately started crying when she heard his voice. It had been over three months since they were last together.

Bill spoke first saying, "Hi Honey" It was such a joy for Sarah to hear Bill's voice again. Sarah began to cry. I grabbed the phone from Bill and quickly said, "Hi Sarah, It's me, Joe" but Bill took it back and said, stop clowning around.

Then Bill continued his conversation with Sarah saying, "I love you and miss you terribly. I do not know when I can come home as we are under strict orders not to say anything about the war or what we are doing. I can say that it looks like we will be relocating to another camp for more training but I don't know when."

Sarah responded by saying, "My heart and prayers are with you as are the prayers of our church. We pray every day for your safe return. Oh, guess what? I have some good news. I got a part time job in a small factory just outside of town and I am pregnant."

Bill stammered and then said. "Did you say you were pregnant?" Sarah said, "That's right. We're going to have a baby." Bill was overjoyed with the news saying, "I am going to be a father. How cool is that?"

I laughed and shouted, that's great; I'm going to be an honorary uncle. Imagine that!

I could hear Bill talking to Sarah saying, "You know what this means, don't you? It means that I have to survive and come home after the war. I hope our baby will be a boy. If it's a girl, she and I will still toss the football around on a Sunday afternoon." Then Bill said, "Ok Sarah, I will do my very best." Then the phone connection began to get static on it and they said their last goodbyes.

Three days later we received our deployment papers. We were to report to the Norfolk Naval Base, Norfolk, VA. It was the world's biggest naval base at that time. That's where the troop transport ships were docked.

The army decided to fly Bill and I to London England from Norfolk with other special forces instead of going by ship. Upon arrival in England we were assigned to set up last minute training.

We had some time off and spent it in the canteen playing cards, throwing darts, and shooting pool. I looked around the canteen and saw two British girls. I listened to them and thought that they spoke funny. They had a strange accent. Bill agreed and kept shooting pool so I, being the single and eligible batcher that I am, asked one of them to dance.

It had been a while since Bill was with Sarah and female companionship would have been nice but Bill's heart was still true to Sarah. He stayed at the pool table with a few other soldiers while I enjoyed the British humor and accents. I realized that flirting was universal and done by men and women all around the world, no matter what country you are in.

We did not know exactly what type of mission we were to go on but it was evident that it was important. We kept seeing new faces and meeting new soldiers from the 1st and 29th army divisions. They arrived by the busload. Everyone felt that there was something big about to happen but we would not even try to guess what.

Bill could not help but remember the terrible nightmare that he had back home when he was with Sarah. He knew a big invasion was close and that he would be thrust into the middle of all out war. He also knew that the Germans were waiting and were holding strategic positions where they had the advantage in a head to head conflict.

I could tell that Bill was drifting back into his memories of that bad dream he told me about on the way to boot camp.

I could see a blank stare in his eyes so I said, "A penny for your thoughts. What's going on?"

Bill came out of his blank stare and decided to share his nightmare with me in more detail. He said, you remember the dream I told you about? Well it's still on my mind. "The last night of my honeymoon I had a nightmare. It was so real that I thought I was pulled into the future.

I saw myself being killed in action on one of the beaches of Normandy. I woke in a cold sweat trembling inside. Now that terrible dream is about to unfold. I know that I am not going to make it through this conflict and certainly not home to Sarah."

I had to cheer him up or he would freeze in battle and really die. I told him, "You can't think that way. Sure, lots of us are going to die but the opposite is also true. Lots of us will live and we will win this war and return home to our loved ones."

The next day, we got orders to board the troop ships that would transport the invasion force. It was time to see if Bill's dream would come true or not. Would he be one of the thousands that died on the beaches of Normandy?

Battle of Omaha Beach

Zero hour had come and the Invasion of Normandy was at hand. It was 4:55 A. M. on June 6th 1944. Over 100,000 Allied troops made it to shore that day. But it was just beginning for Bill and me. We were off loaded from the transport ship into a landing craft. Other ships were doing the same with their soldiers.

As we crowded into the landing craft, I looked at Bill and said,

"Well, here we go. Good luck my friend. God be with us both in our hour of despair." Bill agreed saying, "Lord help us."

After 30 minutes or so, there were hundreds of landing crafts circling the area. Many had already landed on the beaches of Normandy. Bill and I were headed towards Omaha Beach. The seas were up with high winds and waves. The temperature was around 59 degrees.

I said to myself… "Get it together man." Then I cried out to God in my heart saying, "I don't want to die here, I don't want to die."

Nothing went as planned. In the predawn darkness, the crafts carrying the invasion force took longer than expected to form up, and many hit the beach without armor protection. The various waves of landing crafts became mixed up in the confusion.

Every landing craft was taking on water like crazy. Some of the landing crafts began sinking. Those that stayed afloat took enemy fire. Landing crafts were being hit by enemy shells and exploding. Most of the men succumbed to seasickness.

The enemy fire spooked the navy guy driving our boat. He slowed down to a crawl. "Get to the beach!" Bill yelled. "Get this thing going!" His reprimand worked. The navy guy gave it more power. As the boat sped up it hit a floating mine, about 300 yards from the beach.

Bill and I were tossed overboard into a rough sea and a barrage of enemy machinegun fire. We sank to the bottom right away because of the weight of our packs. We struggled for a while and then used our utility knifes to cut loose and surfaced, only to hear bullets flying everywhere.

There was nowhere to go and the water was too deep for us to stand up.

After a few minutes of treading water, we hitched a ride from another landing craft by hanging on for dear life. We moved closer to Omaha Beach. There was supposed to be a signal boat to guide us and other battlefield preparations that would protect us. None of it was there.

There was no control boat out in the water, there were no bomb craters on the beach to use as foxholes, and no one ever saw an Allied plane. The bad weather grounded them.

The only thing we could do is play dead in the water letting the tide bring us into shore. We had already seen other soldiers lift their heads or try to stand up and were immediately shot by enemy snipers.

Then Bill called to me saying, "Come on Joe, let's run for cover near those rocks." In the midst of enemy fire, we ran for our lives as bullets whistled in the air all around us.

"Thank God? I said to Bill. "We are safe for the moment." I looked over at Bill again and said, "Where is the rest of our division?" Bill said, "Who knows? We'll probably see them later today."

Then I looked back over Omaha beach and saw it full of fallen comrades from 20-feet seaward of the water's edge inward as far as the tide had carried them. I knew then within my heart that I was looking at most of our division. We were the lucky ones. So far, we had survived.

I moved over to where Bill was, about 10 feet away and said, "At least your crazy nightmare was just a bad dream and not a vision of the future. You're still here, buddy."

After about an hour, Bill and I met five other soldiers from another company and we slowly crawled and ran to higher ground, killing enemy snipers and destroying stationary machine gun nests along the way.

Finally we reached the 1st of many hedgerows. We stopped to survey the area when enemy fire came at us from several directions. Our makeshift squad of seven men came face to face with an unknown number of German soldiers. I returned fire with support from some of the other men while Bill and two others crawled in a ditch to flank the enemy. Once in position, they killed all the Germans with rapid machine gun fire and grenades.

The five men that joined us on the beach decided to move on towards the first town. We should have gone with them but Bill and I were exhausted and stayed back to rest and regain our strength. We thought it was a safe place to rest.

Finding The Lost Coin

Bill and I were left all alone standing by a hedgerow. I saw a big tree and said to Bill, "Let's rest under that tree. It will keep the sun off of us for awhile." Bill agreed and we sat down to rest. I began to reminisce saying, "Boy, could I have a burger with fries and a cherry coke. Remember that little place Bill, where we hung out together with Sarah and all those other pretty gals?"

Bill replied, "I sure do, Joe" Now Go to sleep, I'll take the first watch."

As I settled down and closed my eyes, Bill pulled his utility knife and began digging in the soil around the tree where he was sitting. He said, "This is a good way to pass the time."

Suddenly Bill unearths a few broken pieces of pottery and a golden coin. He said, "Hey Joe, look what I just found. It's a golden coin." I mutters, "Ok Bill, that's great" and tried to go back to sleep.

But Bill, still being excited said, "No really, it's a golden coin but it is not French. It looks like a Spanish coin." I sat up and said, "What's a Spanish coin doing under a French tree?" Bill said, "Not sure but it must be valuable. The date is in the 17th century." Bill tucked the coin in his wallet and said, "I'll look it up when I get back stateside."

We rested for a few hours. Then Bill said, "Get up Joe. We better move along and catch up to our unit, if it still exists." I said to Bill, "Ok Partner". Then we moved out along the hedgerow towards the first town. It was obvious to me that we were now officially combat commandoes. It was a strange feeling to be ready to kill and ready to die if necessary.

An hour and a half later, we meet up with 20 or so U.S.

Army Infantrymen. As we talked and greeted each other, out of nowhere, the enemy launched a surprise attack and Bill was killed in action by an exploding mortar. I was badly wounded and almost died myself. I would have if it hadn't been for two soldiers that rushed me to a nearby field hospital.

Two other army guys were killed and four were severely wounded. I woke up a week later in that field hospital only to learn that Bill had been killed. My injuries were serious but not life threatening.

The nightmare from the past had apparently come true. Bill was dead and so were his dreams for the future. Bill became another casualty of war in the official records of U.S. Army WW II files. My best friend became a statistic. That was a pill really hard to swallow. More than 37,000 ground forces died in the Battle of Normandy. I felt really bad for months after they told me.

Bill's belongings were gathered together, and sent with his body stateside. Sarah had just given birth to a baby boy when she receives the news that Bill had been killed in action. His body and belongings arrived several weeks later.

Sarah's parents made all the funeral arrangements. The casket was not opened at the funeral because of the mortar explosion. After the funeral, Sarah's mother gave Sarah a small box with Bill's wallet and some other personal things inside. They were found near his body.

All she had was a box and a memory. Tears came into her

eyes. She thought, "What am I going to tell my son as he grows up and asked about his dad?" That's what she told me when I called her from the hospital where I was recovering.

They were high school sweethearts with dreams of the future. He promised her that he would come back home but she didn't really believe it would be in a casket. She vowed that she would never fall in love again.

After many hours of grieving, she put the box on a closet shelf where it remained until Bill Jr. was 10 years old…at which time she proudly gave it to Bill Jr. She said, "You are now old enough to have these memorial items. Take good care of them as they are all that is left of your dad."

Bill Jr.'s Golden Coin

When I last talked to Sarah, she told me the story of her son and a special golden coin. She said that Bill Jr. opened the box and found his dad's wallet. He said, "How can I remember someone that I never knew?" Then he began to look inside the wallet where he saw pictures of his dad with a few army buddies, a military ID, and even a few dollar bills. Then he found a secret compartment.

He shook the wallet hard and a shinny golden coin fell on to the floor. He noticed that it was a Spanish coin by the writing on it and that it was very old.

Sarah didn't know that there was a golden coin until later. Bill Jr. played with the coin every day. He even showed it to his friends and other boys at school but they said it was a fake. Bill Jr. took the coin everywhere and kept boasting how it was a valuable Spanish coin that his dad found in France and that one-day it would make him rich.

He often wondered, "How could a Spanish coin get buried in French soil" No one knew how the coin got there but the mystery was big in Bill Jr.'s mind. He would dream up battles with ships and soldiers with swords and ancient weapons. Having the golden coin brought him closer to his dad because he felt that his dad would have thought the same way.

Several days later a group of boys from Bill Jr.'s school tried to take the coin away from him, again saying he was stupid and the coin was a fake. Bill Jr. pushed one of the boys and ran into the forest. The boys chased after him throwing rocks.

Bill Jr. didn't want the boys to have his dad's coin so he tossed it into the forest saying, in anger, "it's just a stupid old coin." The boys stopped chasing when they saw him toss the coin. However, the golden coin bounced off a tree and landed right in front of a squirrel that grabbed it and ran away.

Bill Jr. chased the squirrel but couldn't catch it. Then he heard a gunshot in a distance and decided to get out of harm's way. He ran home and told his mother what had happened saying to Sarah,

 "Mom, I lost the coin" Sarah said, "What coin?" and Bill Jr. said, "the one that was in dad's wallet. It was a Spanish coin that was   over 300 years old."

Sarah was beside herself and was angry with her son. "Look at me", said Sarah to Bill Jr. "You should have shown it to me right away. Maybe it was worth something. I wonder how your dad got it in the 1st place?" "Maybe we can find it, said Bill Jr. Sarah replied, "Not now, I am too busy and it's getting dark," and so ended the search for the Golden Coin.

Sarah told me that she prayed that night saying, " Dear God, I know we are not suppose to chase after riches but things are getting worse in my finances. Please help me and show me what to do."

Sarah sat on her bed and opened her bible. She didn't know just where to read. Her eyes fell on the 28th verse of Romans in chapter eight. She read the verse out loud saying,

"And we know that all things work together for good to those who love God, to those who are the called according to His purpose."

Sarah said that it was as if God was talking directly to her in response to her prayer. She said that she came to the conclusion that, she loves God and was a Christian, which meant that she was called of God and that qualified her for this special move of God. She really believed that God would work everything together for good, even the bad things that came into her life. They would pass away with time.

Sarah went to sleep that night with a lighter burden than when she started out that day. She had an unusual peace that could only be God's favor upon her.

Now Johnny wanted to know what had happened to the golden coin. I told him that he'd have to wait a bit and it would all come to light and he would know all the details.

Squirrel Hunting

The same squirrel that bill Jr. saw crossed the path of a hunter named Sam that was squirrel hunting in the area. Sam took a shot at the squirrel with his 22-caliber rifle and thought he had hit it. He ran to where the squirrel was but it was gone. All he saw was a golden coin laying on a rock. It sparkled in the sunlight. He picked up the coin and went home without bagging a squirrel that day.

Sam tucked the coin in his wallet and went on his way back to where he lived. The golden coin became a good luck charm for Sam. He liked to show it off every chance he could.

One day his boss asked him to move to a small town just outside of Odessa, TX and to take over that office as its manager. Sam took the challenge and moved to Midland, TX, the small town where the office was located. He would be the new manager of a Real Estate satellite office.

Sam was a Christian and loved people. He quickly found a church and began to volunteer as a youth worker.

Meanwhile Sarah and Bill Jr. moved back to Midland from Odessa to live with her mother as times were hard and she could not make it on her own. Sarah was a single mom. Her vow to not marry was still in force. She had hardly even dated over the past 10-years since Bill Sr. died.

She joined the same church that Sam belonged to and Bill Jr. started attending the church youth group meetings. Sam and Sarah met in church and began dating soon after. This was a hard decision for Sarah because Bill was still her heartthrob and she felt that he could never be replaced. But Sam was very much like Bill and he adored her and loved to spend time with Bill Jr.

Bill Jr. had anger issues that went back to never having a dad. The other kids teased him about it. He and Sam spent many hours together talking and Sam became a father figure to him.

Sam and Sarah dated off and on for three months. She still had problems with dating. Bill Jr. was happy that Sam and his mother were dating. He really liked Sam and hoped that soon he would get a dad…but he was sad that he never knew his real father. He had pictures to look at but it was hard to imagine his dad being with him.

He could only wonder what his real dad was like and if Sam was anything like him. He constantly asked his mother and she told him some stories about when she was with his dad in high school and the 1st year of marriage before he went off to war. She assured him that Sam was very much like his dad.

One night, when Sam and Sarah were on a date, she asked him," where do you hail from? I don't know anything about you."

Sam shared the story of his WW II ordeal, how he was severely wounded in the invasion of Omaha Beach. He told Sarah, "All I can remember is a loud explosion. When I woke up, I was in an army hospital. I suffered severe burns on my face, torso and hands. Plus, I lost my memory due to a brain injury from the blast."

"It is a miracle that I am even alive. I was in the hospital for three years and underwent 14 different operations. Because they had no idea who I was, they could not restore my looks. The plastic surgeons said they would make me handsome but, well, you can be the judge of that."

Sam said he named himself. He picked the name of the doctor that worked on him. His name was Sam and it seemed to fit. Sam said, "Who I really am is still a mystery. I guess I'll never know. The doctor said one day it all will come back to me but that hasn't happened as yet."

Sarah said, "Wow, that is some story. You could have a wife and kids somewhere."

Sam replied, "Not likely, I was barely out of high school.

There wasn't time to marry and have kids. I was just a lonely soldier away from home, I think."

A few weeks later, Sam took Sarah and Bill Jr. to a local ice cream parlor for a dip or two of their new cherry vanilla flavor. While eating ice cream, Bill Jr. asked Sam about his good luck charm and how he got it. Bill Jr. never got a good look at it.

Sam said, "Sure, it is quite a story. I went squirrel hunting one day back before I met you guys. It was a long drive for me to get to the right spot but finally I made it to Odessa, TX. That was supposed to be the best spot. It was famous for the biggest and best tasting squirrel in the country.

I walked many miles through the forest hoping to bag a squirrel. Then I finally saw a big squirrel cross my path and I quickly fired off a round but when I got to where the squirrel was, the only thing I found was a shinny gold coin laying on a rock. It was sparkling in the sunlight."

Bill Jr.'s ears perked up and his eyes got bigger and bigger as he listened to Sam talk about his lucky charm. He asked to see the coin and immediately realized that it was his lost coin. Sarah said, "Where is this place that you were hunting?"

Low and behold, it was the same forest where Bill Jr. lost his golden coin. Bill Jr. jumped in saying, "This coin is mine. It is the same one that I found in my dad's wallet. He demanded that Sam give it back to him."

Sam said, "The golden coin is mine. It has become my good luck charm. I have no interest in letting it go". He also said, laughingly, "it couldn't be your coin because I got it from a squirrel."

Bill Jr. and Sam went back and forth arguing over who owned the coin. Sam said to Bill Jr., "You lost it so you have no more right to it." But Bill Jr. argued, "I tossed it only so the other boys would not get it. I went back later looking for it but didn't find it."

Bill Jr. appealed to his mother for help saying, "Mom, make him give it to me"

Then Sarah put the matter to rest. She said, "If this coin is the same one that God gave to my Bill, then it rightfully belongs to my son." Then she looked into Sam's eyes and asked for the coin.

Sam and Sarah stared at each other for a few more seconds as if to see something in each other's eyes that was not there before…something familiar that was lost and now found.

Sam spoke, laughingly, "Sarah, my darling, you are now my good luck charm. God brought me to you from who knows where but it's a miracle. I no longer need a good luck charm." Sam placed the coin in Sarah's hand which brought back a familiar feeling that he felt somewhere before but he wasn't sure where. Sarah took the coin and put it away for safekeeping.

It Came To Pass

Things often come to pass,
but seldom do they ever last.
They come into our busy day
for a while, and then pass away.

We hear their voices, loud and clear,
when they arrive and while they are here.
They speak both joy and misery,
some to you and some to me.

We say, "It came to pass,"
Or say, "It happened so fast."
Down life's beaten path
comes both love and wrath.

So say goodbye to sad and blue,
to all that is now troubling you.
For things will come, only to pass,
but God's love will always last.

Written By
John Marinelli

Dead? Or Alive?

After Sarah put the golden coin away for safekeeping, she looked again at Sam and said, "What is it about you that is so familiar? I can see it in your eyes and hear it in your voice and even feel it in your touch. Who are you, really?"

Then Sarah reached out and touched Sam, saying, "Oh My God! Are you my Bill?" Could it be? You're so much like him.

Her words hit Sam like a ton of bricks and his head began to ache and his throat dried up and he began to tremble.

"I remember", he cried out in tears. "I remember!", looking at Sarah, "We're married." and, looking at Bill Jr., "You are my son." "I remember our wedding and the gang at Midland High and joining the army and finding the golden coin and being blown up by a mortar in the battle of Normandy.

Sam and Sarah hugged and cried together for quite a while. The realization that Sam was really Bill and Bill was not killed in WW II had to sink in. They spent the next few hours talking about what happened to both of them over the past ten years. Bill Jr. listened and hung on to every word. He wanted to know everything. This was his real dad. He couldn't help but join in on some of the hugs and cry along with Sam and Sarah.

Sarah looked over at Bill Jr. and said, "Honey, Sam is really Bill, your real father. He is the Bill Anderson that was my childhood sweetheart and my husband. They said he died but he didn't. He was lost but we just found him."

Bill Jr. looked back at Sarah and said, "I know. He didn't die in the war? Wow! I have a dad."

Sam changed his name back to Bill and married Sarah again, just to be sure. They had a big wedding with all the now older classmates and their families.

Local Media Intrusion

The local media caught wind of Bill's story and began to research into the matter. They wanted to know who was in Bill's grave at Arlington National Cemetery. They also wanted to know how much Bill remembered that could be verified. He didn't look like Bill and had no fingerprints as a result of the mortar explosion injuries. Normal verification could not be accomplished.

The question of who was buried at Arlington Cemetery could not be known. That body was placed in the Unknown Soldier's section of the Cemetery. (DNA testing did not begin until 1983.)

Mary and I went back to Midland to visit Sarah when we heard that Bill was alive. We met Sam and it did seem strange. He was a lot like Bill. I spoke up and said, "How about a knowledge test where we all ask questions and Bill or Sam answers them." It was decided that Bill's classmates, parents and Sarah be the ones to ask the questions. It got so much attention that the Q & A session was televised on National T.V.

While we were planning the Q & A, Sam was invited to appear on national talk shows and even many radio shows. It became the main news buzz for several days and culminated with a special FOX News Report on prime time T.V. Sam, who was really Bill, became a hero.

The Q & A was the most watched program of that year.

Sarah began the questioning with, "Where is the beauty mark on my body?" Bill replied, "You don't have a beauty mark" "That is correct."

Steve, a former basketball team player asked, "Which position did you play on the basketball team" Bill answered, "I played in every game and my position was forward guard" "That is also correct."

Bill's dad asked, Where was our favorite fishing hole" Bill

answered, "That's easy, we never went fishing because of my basketball schedule and your work" "That's right"

I asked only one question, what's my middle name? Bill had to think a bit on that one but then smiled and said, "Your middle name is "Blank." You don't have one. I used to call you Joey the blank. We laughed about it. Bill was correct. He kidded me often about not having a middle name.

The Q & A session went on for the better part of an hour and Bill never missed a question. He got all of them right.

Sarah decided to ask one last question. She looked right into Bills eyes and said, "Why did you sleep with Suzie? Bill quickly answered, "I Never Had Sex With That Woman" Sarah replied, "Good"

The war department still wanted more proof. The questions were not enough. They were on the hook for 10-years of back pay with potential raises in rank and other benefits.

Bill made it easy for them by saying that they kept Sam alive and spent lots of money and time to ensure his survival. Because Sam was Bill and Bill was Sam, he released the army of any further payments except for his monthly disability payment and the surgical restoration to bring Sam back to looking like Bill.

Bill was declared "Alive" by the local court system. He was able to get his driver's license restored, military status corrected, and all other identification papers back in order.

Sarah's Bill came home from the war. He was alive and in his right mind.

> *Now* **faith is** *the substance of things hoped for, the evidence of things not seen.*
> *Hebrews 11:1*

Mystery of The Golden Coin

Bill looked into the value of the golden coin. He said to Sarah and Bill Jr. "This coin was buried for over 300 years and then found, only to travel across the sea to Bill Jr. so he could toss it into the forest, so a squirrel could steal it away, so I could find it and give it to Sarah.

God didn't cause the hurt and suffering we all went through these past ten years. I was dead and you guys were alone but God was always with you and He was always with me. He was watching over us and causing all things to work together for our good and His purposes. This is a true miracle. The Mystery of The Golden Coin is that God can use anything to accomplish His will, even a golden coin and a squirrel.

Bill and Sarah took the coin to a dealer in foreign coins

and discovered that it was extremely rare. In fact, up to this point there were only three coins with that date in existence. Sarah's coin would be #4. After validating its authenticity, Sarah put the shinny golden coin up for sale.

The boys that chased Bill Jr. calling the coin fake were wrong. Bill Jr. made sure they knew it. Bill and Sarah got more than enough money from the sale of the coin to take care of their new family for a long time.

There was enough to pay for Bill Jr.'s college, Sarah and Bill's remarriage and even put a down payment on a nice home in Midland, TX. Oh yea, and they bought a new car.

Sarah, Bill Sr. and Bill Jr. were amazed at the way God does things. Sarah said, "We can't help but marvel at the way God works in the lives of His children. God is certainly a God of miracles. She said, "My Bill was killed in the war but here he is alive."

"The army said my son would never know his real dad but here they are together." "They said times would be hard for Bill Jr. and me but God has provided financial security for many years to come" It was all because of a shinny golden coin that was lost and found again 300 years later. He surely does work in strange ways."

You all probably think that the story of Bill and Sarah is over. All good things have to come to an end but this story is not over. It's just beginning and there is a lot more to know about my two friends.

Before we continue, I want to tell you that Bill and Sarah are dear to my heart. They have been my best friends from the 6th grade, over 55 years.

Father And Son Bonding

Bill Jr. had a deep bond with Sarah, his mother. It was so special because they were together, without Bill Sr. for over 10 years. It was time now for Bill Sr. and Bill Jr. to get to know each other as parent and child, as buddies and as friends.

Bill Jr. was already somewhat of an outdoors kind of kid. He liked to fish and run through the woods but had no direction as to being an outdoorsman. Bill Sr., on the other hand, was trained in wilderness survival and how to survive the elements. Thus came the camping trips, fishing holes and lakes, hunting and other sports activities.

Bill Jr. became good at living off the grid. He and Bill Sr. bonded and found in each other a true sense of happiness. It was a, "Like Father, Like Son" extravaganza with no holes barred. Sarah jumped right into the middle of it and was a real sport. She went along on most trips and roughed it out with the boys. They all had ten lost years to catch up on and they did.

Bill Jr. learned how to use a bow and arrow, a machete, a 22 cal. rifle and pistol. He was so excited and willing to learn that he practiced continually until he because an expert. He grew up as a man's man, strong in body and mind.

Bill Sr. and Sarah spent a lot of time grooming Bill Jr. to be patriotic, kind to others, polite in public, and most of all true to their Christian values. However, the outside world was a continual threat to Bill Jr. and all the good things Bill Sr. and Sarah wanted for their son.

Bill Jr. was growing up in an imperfect world that was full of immorality, selfishness, lust for power, racial hate and war.

Society was changing. Some would say for the good and other for the bad. God was banished from the pledge of allegiance, government buildings, school textbooks and classrooms. Teen pregnancies were on the increase and abortion because the primary means of birth control.

The Christian values taught by Bill Sr. and Sarah was looked at as old fashioned and antiquated. Secularism was the new norm and being politically correct was how folks were accepted.

Bill Jr. had a hard time trying to stay pure in heart and loyal to his parent's beliefs. Liberalism took hold and led many astray including Bill Jr. He finally succumbed to the sexual revolution and dabbled into the pot culture. Drugs crept into his world and became his Lord.

All of this seemed normal and ok because everyone was doing it. At least that's what the national media said. No one realized that the public trust embedded in the nation's news media had been broken by far left liberals with big bucks. Their slant on immorality slowly infiltrated the living rooms of every American family.

All of a sudden it was ok to be a homosexual, an unwed mother and a drug user. As long as you don't hurt anyone else, it was acceptable. The family structure began to shift to accommodate single moms and drugs on a scale never seen before.

Bill Jr. fought the traditional America and followed the path of new age thinking that led many of his friends to personal degradation and destruction.

Several years went by and Bill Sr. and Sarah prayed for Bill Jr. every night. They couldn't call him because he actually lived off the grid in Alaska as a wilderness guide for adventure seekers.

Finally things came to an abrupt end when Uncle Sam drafted Bill Jr. for service in the Vietnam conflict. His time alone in Alaska under the stars and waist deep in the snow seemed to bring him back towards his parent's teaching.

He found a sense of peace with God and began to read the Bible. The faith and values of his mother and father became his. He began to seek the truth of God's Word.

59

Military Life
2nd Generation

The draft took Bill Jr. and sent him directly to a naval boot camp. They said that the Army and Marines had already met their quotas for that month and the other services were not recruiting at that time. So Bill Jr. ended up in the naval boot camp at Great Lakes IL. Twelve weeks of exercise, running, school and discipline whipped him into shape both mentally and physically. He was now ready to face the world but not before his two year draft was up.

I kept in touch with Bill Sr. and Sarah. They gave me all the details on how things were with Bill Jr. He was assigned to a destroyer out of San Diego, CA. that was headed for Vietnam.

Their assignment was to support marine forces with off shore bombardments north of Saigon. It was a joint exercise with SEATO forces. The joint effort was to take place in the South China Sea.

So there he was in the middle of the ocean with Australian and English war ships playing war until a junior officer of the deck read and execute order to change course.

The officer turned to the left instead of to the right as the command dictated. The two ships collided in a matter of minutes. The USS Frank E. Evans moved directly across the bow of the HMAS Melbourne of the Royal Australian Navy. It was a light air craft carrier.

The Evans was cut in half, with the Bow half sinking in about 2 minutes taking 74 men to a watery grave. There were probably close to 200 survivors either in the water or on the aft section of the ship, which stayed afloat. There were no casualties on Melbourne. It was probably the worst navel sea disaster in modern times.

Bill Jr. saved the lives of two of his shipmates by pulling

them from the twisted metal of the impacted area of the ship. All three men ended up in the sea with many other sailors. Bill Jr. made sure they all had life jackets. For his quick thinking and bravery, he was awarded the Navy Cross.

Bill Jr. and many other survivors were left to tread water for many hours until their rescue. Among the 74 men lost were three brothers that requested assignment together. This was the 1st time the navy allowed the same duty to relatives since the seven Sullivans died in WW II.

Bill Jr. kept telling his friends that God would work everything out for good. One of the men commented saying, "How can you say that with such assurance" Bill Jr. said it was because his mother believed the Bible and she said that was what it said would happen.

Bill Jr. went from being an agnostic in the wilderness of Alaska to a believer in the God of his parents. The fact remained; they were still treading water, watching for sharks and rescue ships.

Bill Jr. told his dad later that the water was very cold. It was hard to stay cognoscente. The other shipmates sustained minor injuries that left a trail of blood in the water.

The HMAS Melbourne of the Royal Australian Navy was badly damaged and had drifted out of sight. It was just after 3:00 AM under a cloudy darkened sky. Bill Jr. took charge and forced the men to move their legs and arms to keep the blood circulating. He kept a sharp eye out for sharks that might be attracted to the blood in the water. They had no life raft, and had to share life jackets as not all had them.

The situation grew worst as the sun rose above the China Sea. The sea began to form white caps and large rolling waves. The sky poured out its thunder and rain. The winds blew as though there was no tomorrow. The shipmates were growing weaker with every hour that passed.

Bill Jr. was at the end of days or so he thought. It would have been easy to just give up and drown but Bill Jr. would not. He, instead, called on God to help him. He remembered what his dad told him before he left home.

Bill Sr. told him, "Son, if you ever get into a jam, where you feel you cannot get out of by your own power, call upon the Lord. He is a very present help in times of trouble."

It was in that moment, when Bill Jr. was about to die, that his parents' faith became his. He called upon the Lord and trusted in God to save him and his shipmates.

Finally, after many hours in the cold China Sea, they all were rescued and placed upon various other ships for treatment or observation.

Bill Jr. started showing signs of P.T.S.D. (Post Traumatic Stress Disorder) The navy sent him back stateside to spend some time with his parents. Bill Jr. had to fight one more battle to regain his peace of mind. His emotional state would keep him from any further combat.

He looked forward to fishing with his dad again and maybe even camping with Sarah and friends.

Bill Jr. and his Asian wife arrived safely home around 9 P. M.

"Hold on Dad", said Mark. "Where did this wife come from? You never said anything about Bill Jr. getting married."

"I was just kidding. I wanted to see if you guys were still listening. How am I doing so far?" Little Johnny spoke up and said, "Great Grandpa." Will someone get me another glass of Iced Tea and I will continue.

I've been telling you the story of Bill and Sarah Anderson, my best friends in the entire world. They demonstrated true love, compassion and friendship by living life with honor and dignity. They lived up to their word and sought to honor God in all that they did.

Tragedy On The Home Front

"What happened next Grandpa?" Said Johnny. Well, said grandpa Joe, Bill Jr. came home for a few months and then came to see Mary and me. He needed a rest from life and our 10-acre hobby farm was just what the doctor ordered.

He spent the better part of a year helping expand our gardens, harvest two fields of corn and doing prep work for spring planting.

However, he grew restless and that fall informed us that he was going back home to his parents. He left that next week. We lost touch with him after that. We pray now and then that God would keep him safe and settle his spirit.

Two years ago this July, Bill Sr. called me sobbing and trying to talk. I tried to calm him down so I could ascertain what had happened. A few minutes later Bill shared with us that Sarah had been seriously hurt in an automobile accident while coming home from the store. Bill was driving when it happened. A drunk driver ran a stop sign and hit their van broadside. It was the passenger's side where Sarah was sitting.

Bill was injured but not seriously. He pulled Sarah from the van just before it burst into flames but she was severely injured. She lay in Bill's arms as they waited for help. The last words she spoke before going unconscious was, "God will work all things together for good, even this… I love you" and then she slipped into a deep comma.

"No!, not Sarah," said Mark. "How could God allow it to happen?" That's what I said, son. How could such a gentle loving soul suffer so much?

As I hung up with Bill Sr. I began to remember what Sarah said to Bill. Everything will be ok because God will work it out. Even in a time of tragedy and great suffering, she held on to God's word. It was the hook that held her faith in place and kept it strong.

I still struggled with, Why Sarah? Why did God let this happen? As I wrestled with God in my thoughts, I remembered what our pastor taught in last week's Bible study. He talked about "Free Will" and how God has given man a free will to do whatever he so chooses.

However, with that free will comes consequences. The pastor quoted a Bible verse that helped us all to better understand. It said,

"Be not deceived; God is not mocked: for whatsoever a man soweth, (or plant) that shall he also reap. (or harvest) For he that soweth (plants) to his flesh shall of the flesh reap corruption; but he that soweth (plants) to the Spirit shall of the Spirit reap life everlasting.

Galatians 6:7-8

I realized that God didn't put Sarah into a comma. The drunk driver did when he chose to drink excessively and drive. Knowing the truth did little to comfort me as I grieved for Sarah and prayed for Bill.

Mary and I went to visit Sarah at the hospital but she was not very responsive. She was on life support and still in a comma. We spent some time with Bill encouraging him to stand strong in the Lord. We both told him that God had a plan and He would work this tragedy out for good. Bill shared with us that Sarah's last words were just that.

Sarah did finally come out of her comma and made a complete recovery. It took a while and there was much suffering through many therapy sessions but it did all work together for good as she said it would. Her faith in God kept Bill calm. He held on to the same promise she received from God many years ago.

Bill and Sarah bought the farm. No, they didn't die. They purchased the hobby farm next door to us and are now our new neighbors.

Sarah told me that Bill Jr. found himself a wife and was living again off the grid in the Alaskan wilderness. He wanted nothing to do with war, society, liberals or politics. He returned to the place where he was happy… before Vietnam. He now had the joy of worshiping God with his new wife under the stars of heaven and that's all that mattered.

Sarah's Path To Recovery

Well look what the cat dragged in? It's Bill and Sarah from the farm next door. Join us! We're just finishing up a rather long story about my two best friends in the entire world.

"Oh" said Bill. "Who might that be?" Joe continued with, "Family? This is Bill and Sarah Anderson. They are the folks that I have been talking about for the last 2 1/2 hours."

There is one thing that we all want to know that only Sarah could tell us. So I asked her, "How did you ever survive that awful car accident? Mary and I visited you when you were deep in that comma and it looked like you would not come out of it. You were in that state of mind for over three months, right?" Please tell us about it.

Sarah began to tell her story and what a story it was. She said, "Well, there I was in a lot of pain and slowly slipping away…to where, I did not know. I remember whispering to Bill that God would work even this out for good…and then I fell into a comma."

"My mind kept thinking about a particular Bible verse. I could not get away from it. Let me say that people do think and even see things while in a comma. They can even hear what people are saying in their hospital room."

Mary asked, "So what Bible verse were you hearing?" "Oh," said Sarah, "It wasn't just a remembering. It was like a booming voice from eternity that said, *"Speak those things that are not as though they were."* I didn't understand at first. I said to God, "I don't understand."

Then I heard the voice again but this time it was a soft voice, almost like a whisper. It said, "Don't accept what you see or feel but believe what I have said in my Word."

"My mind pondered these things all the time I was asleep. Over and over I remembered and wondered how I was to accomplish what God spoke to me. It wasn't until I woke up that I realized the weight of what I heard in the comma."

"I was weak and could hardly talk. I was able to whisper a little and I asked Bill to find the scripture that God spoke to me. Here's how it reads in the King James Version."

> *"(As it is written, I have made thee a father of*
> *many nations,) before him whom he believed,*

even God, who quickens the dead, and calls those things which be not as though they were."

Romans 4:17

"The Bible verse tells the story of when God spoke to Abraham and said to him that he was now the father of many nations. God called that which did not exist into existence. He spoke of it as though it did exist. God said it and that made it so, even if it was not as yet visible."

"I realized that God is speaking to all His children through the Bible. He has already spoken in precious promises that cannot be revoked. They are sure to happen as long as we believe. That was what Abraham did. He believed."

"The doctors told Bill that I would probably never walk again and that I would most likely be slow in mind and speech. However, they didn't know what God was telling me. So, I began to believe what I read in the scriptures. Well, I didn't read. Bill read them to me."

Three Bible promises really stood out to me when I heard them. They are:

"for he hath said,
I will never leave thee, nor forsake thee."

Hebrews 13:5

"Who his own self bare our sins in his own body on the tree, that we, being dead to sins, should live unto righteousness: by whose stripes ye were healed."

I Peter 2:24

But Jesus beheld [them], and said unto them, with men this is impossible; but with God all things are possible.

Matthew 19:26

"I knew then that God had spoken into my spirit and let me know that I was not alone and that I am already healed by the stripes (Death) of Jesus on the cross. He spoke what was not as though it was. All I had to do is what Abraham did, believe it… and I did."

"The doctors were astounded at the progress I was making. Yes, I was in speech therapy and had to learn to walk all over again but I did it with three promises from God."

"It's a great feeling to know that God is on your side."

"He Is My Greatest Fan."

"So that's my story and I am sticking to it. God said it. I believed it and that settled it."

"I still have difficulties at certain times of the day but I always hold on to what God told me just before Bill went off to war. God gave me another scripture that has set the course of my life and helped me to stay in faith."

Joe said, "and what is that verse? As if I didn't know" "Sarah repeated it saying,

"I know that I can count on God to make things right, no matter what."

Bill Jr. And The Grizzly

"So", said Joe, "How's Bill Jr.?" Bill Sr. spoke up to answer the question.

"My son, the bum…lost in the wilderness of Alaska again. You'd think he'd call or write once in a while. However he did call us about six months ago. We talked for almost an hour, at my expense. You know that he was a wilderness guide before Vietnam. Yah, he took people on guided adventures into the Alaskan Bush. Now he just traps, grows his own food and hunts."

"He is living as though it was the 18th century with no electric, no neighbors except for a few Indians and no real job. He barters for things and sells his furs or extra crops if the growing season is good. It's a rough life and he loves it?"

Mary asked Bill, "What about his wife? We know nothing of her?"

Bill Sr. looks at Joe and says, "She's another story. They met at a karaoke bar and hit it off right away. Apparently she can sing, among other things. She is around 5' 1', shapely, brown hair, greenish eyes with tattoos all over her arms and legs. She goes by the name, "Toni." Ain't that a kick in the head? She has a boy's name but with an "I" instead of a "Y" at the end. Bill Jr. said she was from the Bronx, NY where all the tough gals live."

"Well, she's a pretty little thing and tough as nails. Bill Jr. says she chops wood, handles the garden, cooks most of the meals, and even hunts with him. They are a perfect couple, both nuts."

"Bill Jr. had to tell me how Toni saved him from a Grizzly. He first had to give me all the stats on this kind of bear. He said, "There are currently about 55,000 wild grizzly bears located throughout North America, most of which reside in Alaska.""

"Bill Jr. and Toni were hunting and a grizzly came into their camp and attacked Bill Jr. before he could get to his riffle. Toni was already up because it was near sunrise and she was cooking. The smell of food must have drawn the grizzly near."

"Well Bill Jr. ran and as he ran he yelled for Toni. The bear roared and stood straight up. He was over six and a half feet and looked to be about 650 pounds. As the bear came down he swatted at Bill Jr. with his paw and lunged forward towards him."

"Toni grabbed Bill Jr.'s gun and fired off two shots at the bear. She did not aim to hit the bear, only to scare it away and she did. Bill Jr. saw the grizzly run as he held his arm that was somewhat shredded in the encounter."

He made light of it but it was serious. His flesh was ripped from his arm and in some spots the wounds went deep to the bone. But, he survived as he always does. However, all the credit goes to Toni who just happened to have had EMS training back in the Bronx and knew exactly what to do.

Life In The Alaskan Bush

Bill Sr. continues, "The Alaskan Bush is a wild place. Life is hard and few make it that come from the lower 48. Bill Jr. is one of the exceptions."

"Their homestead is in the interior close to Fairbanks with temperatures that dip into the minus 50-degree range. Storms snow them in frequently. Winter power outages come with the territory. Winter is a solid five months out of the year."

"The mid-summer weather is usually nice, in the 70s. The sunsets briefly around midnight but the skies never truly darken. However, the reverse is true for winter months. Folks live in the dark every day."

"The cost of living is definitely higher and is even worse as you go deeper into the more remote areas. The state has a very laid-back feel to it. I guess that's why Bill Jr. likes it so much."

"The bush of Alaska is definitely a different lifestyle. It is nothing like the cities in the lower 48 states. It is truly a "Last Frontier State.""

"Bill Jr. has spent the better part of 3-years building a homestead. He has solar heat, underground coolers to store food and perishable supplies and a natural freezer in winter right at his door. He now owns 50 acres of shear wilderness full of snakes, bears, fox, wolves, and rabbits, birds of all kinds and even deer and moose. His closest neighbor is an hour and a half by snow mobile."

"The fishing is great with Salmon, Trout, Northern Pike and a lot more. They even have a special storage place to salt and store fish for the winter."

"It's not a lifestyle that Sarah and I would desire. It's too cold, too far from civilization and too expensive to live. We'll leave that up to Bill Jr. and Toni."

"Well that's about it. No more to say now. We are all alive and well by the grace of almighty God. It's a good feeling to be at peace with God and those around you."

> ***"In all thy ways acknowledge him,***
> ***and he shall direct thy paths."***
> **Proverbs 3:6**

Our story continues on an overland express bus trip. It

came to pass with a Mysterious Stranger that touched the lives of Bill & Sarah, Joe and several other passengers.

Grandpa Joe speaks up, "Wait, we are not finished with the story." Times were tough back then and full of anxiety. Jealousy, hate, selfishness and anger ruled in the hearts of the proud. Equality would have to wait its turn as life pushed its way into the future.

Time had passed over the years since the Vietnam War came to town but the events that took place were not forgotten.

I can still remember the sunsets and the rippling of the water as the wind blew across the lake. I can also remember that awful night when it rained so hard that mudslides took half of our mountain road. ***This is where our story continues***. Let me tell you about my mystery man.

The Mystery Man And The Bus Driver

The bus was late the night the mystery man arrived. It was after three A.M. There was a lot of fog and few people at the bus station. But I was there because I had business to attend to the next day. I didn't want to drive so I took the overnight express bus. We had 600 miles of open road before arriving at our destination. There was plenty of time to observe this mystery man. I even talked with him for about a hundred miles.

Mark speaks up and says, "Why was he so mysterious? Joe continues, "You'll see as I continue with the story."

Where was I, Oh Yea, His name was no different than any-one else's name. His dress was subdued and pretty much ordinary. He was a tall, dark and somewhat handsome man with broad shoulders. He was soft spoke and his voice comforting. His bearded face made him look tough like a truck driver but when he spoke, you knew he was a gentle man.

He quickly became everybody's friend on the bus and yet nobody really knew him. Folks painted a portrait in their minds of what they wanted to see. They seem to project their mental image on to him. They believed their own lies to suit their own needs. Who he really was, was mine alone to know. For some unknown reason he allowed the bus driver and me to see him as he really was.

He got on the bus at the beginning of the line and traveled with me to the end of the line. We talked about a lot of things from the weather to the future.

His kindness and soft-spoken nature made it easy for me to share things about myself that I had long since forgotten. It was as though I was being "X-Rayed" and those sad and hurtful feeling from yesteryear just dissolved away as we discussed them. Time itself seemed to stop; yet I know that didn't happen.

The Stranger And The Young Married Couple

He left the bus with a young couple that just got married and they all entered the bus station. He had no carryon luggage or suitcases, just himself.

I check in and picked up my luggage and looked for the stranger to say goodbye but he was nowhere to be found. The young couple told me that they turned their back to him to find a seat and when they turned around, he was gone. All they said was that this man told them to name their baby Joseph after the Joseph in the Bible. That was a shock to the couple because they had no idea she was with child.

The Stranger & The Waitress

I sleepily wandered into the only, "All Night" diner where I sat down at the counter and ordered a cup of coffee. The diner was empty except for the waitress and me. She asked me where the bearded man went. I said, "There was no such man in the diner when I entered."

"Wait a minute," she said. "I talked with him for over three hours. He said he was waiting for a bus." I quickly let her know that my bus was the last of the night. The next bus won't leave until 7 A.M.

Then I began to inquire as to his dress and overall looks. She described the man to me and her description was exactly the same as the bearded man on the bus I just got off of…even his eyes were the same color.

How could the same man be talking to this young waitress and me at the same time? I was determined to solve this mystery…so I asked the waitress what they talked about. Here's what she said. *"It's none of your business."* Then she refreshed my coffee.

I couldn't let it drop there, with her abrupt response, so I told her about the bearded man that rode with me on the bus for six hundred miles and the hour we talked to each other directly. After listening to me, she opened up and told me that her bearded man encouraged her to go back to her husband and that God would heal their marriage. She was puzzled as to how this mysterious stranger could know things about her.

The Stranger And The Truck Driver

Then a truck driver came into the all night diner looking for some food and rest from the road. He sat next to me and we struck up a conversation. He told me about a hitchhiker that he picked up a few miles back. Don't you know? It was the same bearded man that talked to the waitress and rode my bus. At least we thought it was.

The truck driver said the guy was nice. He spoke in a quiet

sort of soft voice that kept him from falling asleep at the wheel. He said his bearded man wanted to wait in the truck while he came in for some coffee and a bite to eat.

When I heard that he was still in the truck, the waitress and I ran outside to see if he was the same bearded man that we encountered but he was gone…no where to be found.

We went back inside and talked to the truck driver at length. Everything he said about his bearded man fit our bearded man to a tee. The truck driver said that if it weren't for his rider, he would have crashed because he had been driving for hours and was really tired but didn't want to stop on an isolated road in the middle of the night.

Talk of Angels

There we all were huddled together in an all night diner talking about a mysterious stranger with a bearded face. A waitress, a truck driver, a young married couple, a bus driver and me, strangers unto each other with one thing in common, a mysterious bearded man.

Suddenly, we could see the sunrise peeking through the morning haze and could hear the chirping of little birds as the long night turned into another day. There was a nip in the air and storm clouds off in a distance.

We spent the entire night from the time we pulled into the bus station until the sun rose up to say hello talking about the stranger and how he had helped all of us in some small or big way.

Some of us concluded that the stranger was a ghost in our imaginations, born out of a lack of sleep and loneliness.

Others said the stranger was an angel sent from God to help us in our times of need. I guess we will never really know who the stranger was and how he appeared in all our lives at the same time. All we could say is that our hearts burned inside.

It was as if we knew him but couldn't recall his name. We'd seen him somewhere before but where we could not remember.

Today, Somewhere In Time

It's been over 30-years since we were all together in that "All Night" diner.

The waitress went home to her husband and became a fine mother to three kids.

The truck driver went on to own his own business and stopped pushing himself to the point of exhaustion.

The young married couple did in fact name their 1st child Joseph after the Biblical character. We all wondered how he knew that the child would be a boy before the mother became pregnant.

Then there was the bus driver. He drove that bus for another 15 years and finally retired to Florida where he met a beautiful lady from New York who graciously accepted his invitation to marry. They now have two teenagers.

I believe that the "Mysterious Stranger" was not mysterious at all. I think he was a messenger from God. I could feel the love of God flowing from him as he spoke. I could see compassion in his eyes. It had to be a divine intervention.

All of our lives were dramatically changed from the encounter with the "Mysterious Stranger". You never know who will enter your life and what will happen as a result of a chance meeting. I guess it's good to be hospitable to strangers for they just may be ministering angels from heaven.

"Be not forgetful to entertain strangers: for thereby some have entertained angels unawares."

Hebrews 13:2

Out of Nowhere

And it came to pass that the son of the bus driver was out of control, sliding recklessly toward a terrible future. The bus driver shared his son's story when we spoke by phone the other day.

The bus driver said that it was a gray day with rain in the forecast. The year was 1952. His son's old car needed breaks but he couldn't afford to fix what was wrong. His son was late for work and in a real hurry so, like most law-abiding citizens, he picked up speed and exceeded the legal limit.

Wouldn't you know that the long arm of the law reached out to him with red lights flashing and his siren sounding?

The teen knew he could not get away but he was at an intersection facing a green light turning red. So he sped up faster to get through the light hoping the police officer would stop for the light.

Suddenly, another vehicle turned right in front of him. He came out of nowhere and was in no hurry. He hit the breaks but couldn't stop. Instead he slid through the inter-section burning rubber all the way.

He knew he was wrong but it was just too late. He was about to slam into the side of a brand new Cadillac with little children inside. They were sitting on the side of the immanent impact.

All he could do is cry out to God in hopes that He would help in some way so the children in the car would not get hurt. It wasn't much of a prayer. It was more of a desperate attempt to avoid the consequences of his actions.

He couldn't help but think, "Why would God take the time to help me? My dilemma was a portrait of my life. I was also out of control and running to avoid life's many challenges."

He said that he felt that the world would be a better place if he weren't around. His friends were all on drugs. His 16th birthday had just passed him by without even a "Hello"

There was no reason to strive for excellence like his dad always told him. He tried real hard but look at him. He was just a bus driver's kid. He kept feeling, *"Is That All There Is?"* There had to be more but more of what?

He said that he closed his eyes and waited for the crash but it seemed to be stuck in the moment. He opened his eyes again to see his car sliding in slow motion and slowing down to almost a dead stop.

> *"The angel of the LORD encamps round about them that fear him, and deliver them."*

Psalm 34:7

At the same time, he saw a shadow of a man standing just outside his side window. He had his hand on his car. He could also see the Cadillac racing at full speed in front of him as he slowly slid through the intersection.

Now the policeman stopped at the light, waited for it to turn green and continued to come after the bus driver's son. He finally came to his senses and pulled into a shopping center parking lot and stopped.

Yes, he was given *"The Idiot of The Day"* award and received a reckless driving ticket. The police officer also gave him a long lecture on the law. He scolded the boy and fussed at him and swore on his badge if he ever caught him speeding again, he would throw him under the jail, never mind in jail.

Then he said something strange. He asked the boy if he saw that man in the middle of the intersection. He said that it looked like he was holding the car back while the Cadillac passed. He actually saw what the bus driver's son saw in that slow motion moment.

We both new that there was no way he could have missed hitting the Cadillac. Nevertheless, he missed it and avoided an accident.

The boy told the officer that he also saw the man but when he looked again, he was gone. The officer said it was probably just a guy crossing the street at the wrong time.

We knew better. His dad and I believed that it was God answering the boy's halfhearted prayer. I couldn't help but wonder if the man in the intersection was the, "Mysterious Stranger" that his dad and I met fifteen years ago.

The boy's dad went to court with him to face the consequences of his actions. The judge was amazed that a parent would show up in support of his teen. He told the boy's dad that most of the kids in trouble come alone and have a bad attitude. They do not want their parents to know what they have done.

The judge reduced the charge to speeding and gave the boy a suspended sentence. That meant he didn't have to pay anything but if he ever showed up in his court again he would throw the book at him. The teen wasn't quite sure what that meant but he was glad to be going home.

His dad told the judge that he did not approve of his son's actions and had taken his driving privileges away except to go to school and work after school. He meant it too. He was grounded for two months.

Later that night the teen talked to his mom about his experience. It was quiet in the house. His sister was at a sleep over with a girl friend and his dad was on another bus run. She wanted to know all about what happened and particularly about the man in the intersection.

Here's what he said, "Mom and I talked about everything except sex. We were close and she was not judgmental. She always offered some sort of counsel."

"I told her all about the "Mystery Man" and she was amazed. She said that it had to be the hand of God." Well that opened the door for the teen to express his feelings. He told his mother how he felt all alone and useless.

He had no vision of a future or reason to go on. Yet the encounter with the man in the intersection made him think. Why would God save him from certain death or at least serious injury? He said, "God must want something from me or have something for me that I haven't see as yet."

His mom told him about her feelings as a teen. She said that she too felt empty and useless. She would often think that there was no point to living until she gave her life and heart to Jesus.

The teen responded, "Now I knew some of the religious kids at school and I don't want to be like them. They are always trying to live by a set of rules and regulations that, in their own eyes, make them superior to others around them."

He called these kids, "The Holier-Than-Thou Gang." Life is too hard to be a "Thou Shalt Not" disciple. But his mom said that she was not a, "Thou Shalt Not" type of person. Instead, she relied on what Jesus did and believed in Him as God's only Son. She found happiness and the will to live through God's grace."

So life began to make sense. The boy could be himself and know that God still loved him. He liked what he heard.

So the boy went on with his life. He started going to church and became a member of the youth group. He began to read the Bible and it was there that He met Jesus. He learned of Him and he made Him Lord of his life. He was now His disciple, walking not by laws of religious dogma but by grace.

His dad and I still wondered if the man in the intersection was the, "Mysterious Stranger" that we met many years ago.

Sarah's Tea For Two

Joe continues the story of Bill and Sarah… "There was a reporter that was interviewing folks that saw the mystery man. Sarah, my friend, was one of the folks he interviewed. Here's what the reporter told me. He gave me the full story from start to finish.

Hello, Mrs. Anderson? This is Tom Curry from the Daily News. I was given your name and phone number by a bus driver when I was traveling across country.

The bus driver and I got to talking about angels and He told me a story about you. Could I drop by and interview you for our paper? There's a lot of interest in the supernatural these days and our readers would find your story most interesting.

Mrs. Anderson, in a soft voice, replied, "Please come over. I'll put on a pot of tea."

We sat down on a Sunday afternoon to talk about angels. It was then that I realized that she and her husband Bill were the subjects of a book based on a true love story during WWII.

We talked about how Bill was presumed dead, killed in action, but showed up 10 years later and how a 1700s golden coin brought them back together. The Mystery of The Golden Coin was published to tell their story.

However, the purpose of our "Tea For Two" visit was not their story but hers, when she was seriously injured in an automobile accident. After all the loss and suffering she went through with Bill, then this diagnosis of never being able to be normal again was devastating. She just kept getting worse and medical assistance was of no avail.

My story was not about her accident but the faith that got her through it. What was it about her faith that made the difference? How can faith do anything? What power does faith have to heal? I was hopping that Sarah could shed some light on the subject.

As we talked, Sarah began to cry. She had no clinical answers. She could not tell me the magic ingredient that saved her from becoming a cripple.

I needed answers and she didn't have any. All she had was a simple belief in God and a promise from the scriptures. She had no special formula, no hidden meditational cure and no secret chants. All she had was a God that no one can see and a Bible scripture that most folks never read.

I said to Sarah, "You mean that you were healed by your faith in God?" She quickly replied, "Yes, that is exactly right" Then she went on to explain.

The Bible says that faith is not just a feeling but it is rather a substance. It has shape and will form those things that we hope for. In my case, my faith became the substance of what I desired which was complete healing.

Wait, there's more. Faith was not only the substance of my hope but it was also the evidence of those things that I could not yet see. That means I can rest from all my worry, knowing that my faith will bring forth what I do not see with my eyes, which is life where death is now. You can read it for yourself in Hebrews 11:1.

This Bible scripture was just one that was given to me. The man that gave it also shared several others and told me that they were hooks to hang my faith on.

I asked Sarah, "Who was this Mysterious Man?" but she didn't know. She just said that a man came into her hospital room in the middle of the night and called her by name. According to Sarah, he said in a loud voice, "Sit up Sarah, Your faith has made you whole."

Sarah said that she thought the Mystery Man was an angel because she looked away for a split second and then back again only to find him gone. Now that would be almost impossible because he was too far from the door to have just walked out un-noticed.

She did remember that he said to her, "If you can only believe, you will live and not die" All she knew was that he was there in the middle of her room at the end of her bed and then he wasn't.

According to Sarah, the very next day her levels began to rise and her health slowly improved. It took a while but she did recover completely.

My curiosity got the best of me. I wanted to know the other scriptures that the Mystery Man told her. Sarah said she would be glad to share one more. It was her favorite scripture in the entire Bible. It was the hook that she hung her faith on during WWII.

> *"And we know that all things work together*
> *for good to them that love God, to them who*
> *are the called according to his purpose."*

Romans 8:28

She kept telling herself and everybody else that even though this was a terrible thing, God is working it together for her good because she loved Him and was called according to His purposes.

It didn't matter to Sarah if she lived or died. She believed that God knew best. Her life and times were in His hands to do whatsoever He so desired. However, she had the angel's challenge to believe and be healed so she figured that God wanted her to live. So she believed and lived and is here today with her husband that was declared dead in the war but lived to tell about it.

Sarah said, "Sometimes it is better to see with the eyes of Faith than with the eyes of our understanding. I guess that is because our understanding is finite or limited to our own experiences. Faith, on the other hand, has no boundaries and is not proportionate to that which stands in our way."

Jesus said it this way,

" I say to you, if you have faith as a mustard seed, you will say to this mountain, 'Move from here to there,' and it will move; and nothing will be impossible for you. "

Matthew 17:20

Then Sarah explained, "The mustard seed is very small and the mountain is very large. The difference is that the faith of a mustard seed has the power of God in it and the ability to grow and multiply into an endless source of strength."

Joe And The Reporter

So here I am talking with the great Tom Curry, a newspaper reporter following a "Mysterious Stranger" who helps people in need. The only problem is, they can't absolutely say their helper was an angel. Tom kept hearing stories like these:

A mysterious man that saves someone in harms way, but as soon as the person is safe, the mystery man vanishes into thin air.

A young woman was walking to her car at night after a fun-shopping spree when two men attack her. Their attack is spoiled and they are arrested. The two attackers later admitted that they stopped and ran because of the two big men that suddenly came to her rescue. The young woman saw no men at her side.

A little boy and mother are prevented from getting on a bus by a strange intense-looking man in white clothes who said, "Don't get on this bus" The bus doors close, and it pulls out into traffic and was immediately hit by a tractor trailer, killing everyone on board. But no one else saw the man in white and he was nowhere to be found.

The D-Day miracle was one of the best to date. Tom interviewed Bill Anderson, my best friend and World War Two hero. Here's how his interview went.

So Bill, tell us about your heroic deeds during the big war.

Bill replies, "There isn't much to say and I am not really a war hero."

Tom, "Didn't you shield a squad of men from a mortar attack?" You're a survivor of the Normandy Invasion. You were also a Navy Seal, right?"

Bill, "No I was an Army Ranger, Special Forces. You're thinking of my son Bill Jr. He was the Navy Seal. In fact, he was awarded the silver star after saving several of his shipmates when their ship collided with another."

Tom, "so let's talk about you first. How did you ever survive that mortar attack inland from Omaha Beach?

Bill, "I didn't. All I remember is hearing a blast. I was standing right in the spot where the mortar landed. It should have blown me to bits."

Tom, "But it didn't, why"

Bill, "I think it was because of the prayers of my wife and our church. When the explosion began, I saw a "Mysterious Stranger" dressed in all white. He grabbed me and pulled me toward him. He took the brunt of the explosion. I was severely injured but pretty much in one peace."

Tom, "So it was an angel that saved you that day, right?"

Bill, "Yes and No because the blast blew away most of my face, my hands were badly burned and I lost my memory."

"The mystery man saved my life but the army doctors had no idea whose life it was and I couldn't tell them because of the trauma I suffered in the blast. Even my fingerprints were gone. My clothing was shredded. My military ID and dog tags were gone. Nobody knew who I really was, not even me."

Tom, "What can you tell me about the Mysterious Stranger?"

Bill, "Not much, he was about my height and general build. He was very strong because he pulled me away in a split second before the first mortar hit. He had to have had supernatural strength to do what he did.

I believe that I was saved because of the many and continual prayers of my family and friends back home. They offered up prayer before the throne of God every night and some two or three times a day."

Tom, "What happened then?

Bill, "The Mysterious Stranger tossed me through the air

in the direction of several other rangers that did not get hit. One was a field medic on his way to the triage.

This medic carried me on his back for three and a half miles. He thought I was dead when he laid me on the operating table because I was hardly breathing, had lost a lot of blood and was not moving.

Tom, "What happened to this man in white, the mystery man?"

Bill, "He was all around the area, I was in and out of consciousness and every time I'd wake up, he would be there helping a ranger to go on or a medic to stay focused. He even dropped in on me several times to be sure I was ok. He was the real hero of WWII, not me."

Tom, "Yea, but I can't interview him."

Bill, "I think he was sent by God to help our men in battle. I can even remember seeing him on the beach when sniper bullets were zinging by. Those guys had scopes on their rifles and we are dead center in their sites. There was no way they could have missed; yet they did. It just shows me how the hand of God was there to keep us alive."

Tom, "What about all the men that died that day? Did they not get an angel from God?"

Bill, "No, I think there were many angels but many on both sides of the war still died. I believe this was because war was not God's plan for mankind. He didn't cause it to happen. However, to protect man's free will to choose, He had to let it play out.

As tragic as it was, men had to die as a result of many nations' choices. But God still has a plan for man and knows the future. He listens to His children when they cry out to Him and He respects the many prayers of a community that reverences Him.

Who lives and who dies is in God's hands. We may never know why I lived and my fellow rangers did not. That is another mystery to be revealed in His timing."

There are many Biblical examples of angelic encounters. They are often used as proof text, that God can and does use angels to accomplish His will. What we don't know is why some folks see angels and others do not.

It is quite possible that many people today have entertained an angel without realizing it. The most referred to scripture concerning angels walking among us is Hebrews 13:2

> *"Be not forgetful to entertain strangers: for thereby some have entertained angels unawares."*

It is obvious that angels are in our midst. Their mission is to help us get through tough times. All the more reason we should be nice to strangers and seek to be a blessing. One day, a messenger may visit us.

Tom tells Joe, "Well, that is my report. It will run in tomorrow's paper. What I didn't say in my article was my personal encounter with what I believe was an angel. I couldn't bring myself to admit the existence of God and Angels."

"You see I am a liberal diehard atheist. God is just not in my world. At least I thought that way until I listened to all these fine folks and actually read the Biblical references. But it was my own experience that opened my eyes to the possibility of God. I had to write my article with an acknowledged slant in God's favor.

However, afterwards, at a local bar where newspaper reporters hang out, I met the mysterious stranger. He was seated at the bar.

I say, "Mysterious" because his clothing was old fashioned. It looked like he just stepped out of the 18th century. He even had a pocket watch that was an antique.

Well he kept looking at his watch and then at me. He seemed like he was in a hurry but didn't leave the bar. I couldn't stand the suspense so I went over to him and sat down at the bar. He immediately said, "You're late." I said in response, for what?

The stranger said, "Stick with me. Things are about to get rough." Suddenly the doors opened and three men ran into the bar shooting pistols at anyone in their way. They were yelling something in a foreign language.

The stranger and I were at the very end of the bar so it

took a few minutes to get to us. All of a sudden I was face to face with a terrorists who was bent on killing everyone.

I screamed, "Please don't." It was then that this "Mysterious Stranger" stepped in front of me and took the brunt of their attack. They emptied two magazines into him, one bullet after another.

They kept shooting because the stranger didn't fall. He just stood there in front of me with a big smile on his face. The bullets just bounced off of him.

The police were on the scene really fast but not fast enough. Eight people were killed and four seriously wounded. They shot and killed the three terrorists in a gun battle, all the time with me at the bar behind the mysterious stranger.

When it was all over, the two police officers asked me how it was that I did not get hit. I said, "It was because of him" and pointed in the direction of the mystery man but he was no longer there.

The two cops said that there was no one else but me at the bar. They swore that I was alone from the time they entered the bar.

The "Mysterious Stranger" just vanished into thin air. I know he was there and I could feel the bullets hitting his chest. It was then that I renounced my allegiance to Atheism and became a God-Seeker. I began to read the Bible and saw this scripture;

"Fear not; for I am with you: be not dismayed; for I am your God: I will strengthen you; yes, I will help you; yes, I will uphold you with the right hand of my righteousness."

Isaiah 41:10

Bill Jr.'s Confession

Then Joe began to tell us about Bill Jr.'s confession to Tom, the reporter. He said that they spoke by phone about things and Bill Jr. began to share his deepest feelings.

Bill Jr. said, " I am sorry. I just could not take it anymore. The Vietnam War took it all away, my hopes, my dreams and even my will to live. My dad is the WWII combat hero, Bill Anderson. I am his son Bill Jr.

I grew up learning survival techniques from my dad. He was an expert shot and was trained in how to survive in any condition.

I was more at home off the grid than in the city. The outdoors was my kind of life. I was deep into camping, fishing and hunting. I would go on fly-ins with a buddy to the most remote areas of Montana, Canada and Alaska and spend weeks in God's beautiful nature. I was indeed a "Wilderness Man."

Well now you know pretty much all there is to know about me except for that time I got lost in the Alaskan Bush. There were two weeks that I was lost in the bush. They were more traumatic than being in combat in Nam and treading water for hours in the north China Sea when my ship collided with another.

It's really scary to be in unfamiliar territory and not know which way was the way home. I had always known before but this time I just couldn't figure it out.

I had two different encounters with brown bears and had to run for miles to escape a wild pig that attacked me. Wherever I was, it was a dangerous place.

After several days of searching for a way out of the bush, I realized that I might be here for a while. The only thing to do was to make a base camp and protect myself from the weather. It was the end of spring and fall was just about three miles away.

It took me a few days to get my base camp in order. Then came the snow and bitter cold. Nights dropped down in temperature to a minus 30 degrees. I was in big trouble.

This was supposed to be a two-week adventure in the Alaskan Bush. However, it has quickly turned into a life or death struggle.

It all started when I went down stream chasing after a deer with my trusty bow and arrow. All my survival gear was in the cabin.

The deer ran into the bush and I followed, not aware that the bush was so thick that after a half-mile or so you could no longer hear the river or see through the trees. I tried to get back to the river but the more I wandered the further I went in the wrong direction.

All I had with me was a bow, six arrows and a field knife. The forest was dry and I could hear thunder off in a distance. That was not good as it sets up the possibility for a wild fire. Lightening strikes began to fall and actually blow up trees around me.

How I longed to be with my dad again in a safe environment. We use to sit around a campfire and sing songs and talk for hours about what to do if I were to ever get lost in the forest. All that knowledge would come in handy now. "If I could just remember."

So there I was in the middle of a lightening storm with bolts of electricity from the clouds splitting trees and hitting the ground all around me.

Suddenly a wild fire broke out and the wind blew it my way. I was engulfed in a firestorm. I couldn't run because there was nowhere to run without hitting a wall of flames. It was obvious that this was to be the place of my death.

So I sat down and began to pray that God would take me quickly so I would not suffer long. I asked forgiveness for my many sins and prayed that He would receive me into His kingdom.

The fire closed in and it was hot. I could feel the hairs on my head starting to singe. I closed my eyes and waited for whatever was next.

Then, out of nowhere, a man appeared. He came right out of the flames yet was not burned. He extended his hand to me and said, "Come with me and stay as close as you can." So I did just as he said. We went directly into the wall of flames that was about to consume me but the fire had no affect.

We walked slowly through the fire to safety. When it was all over, we were at the river's edge. The "Mysterious Stranger" pointed to the north and said, "Your cabin is that way, about two miles." I looked down the river and then back his way to say, "Thank You" but he was gone.

I was trembling inside but happy too. I came to the Alaskan Bush for an adventure and certainly got one. I couldn't wait to get back to civilization where I could call my dad and tell him what happened.

It was then that I made the decision to learn all I can and return to Alaska to live off the grid. I knew it would be a real challenge and that's what I was looking for.

Eventually, I made it back but not before finding a wife that was just a crazy as me. We now are Alaskan Wilderness Guides taking city folk on two-week adventures into the Alaska Bush.

This is the place of my dreams and where I will dwell with my family. Life is good and God's grace is even better.

Grandpa's Diary

Bill and Sarah Anderson were cleaning out their attic in preparation to pack and move to Florida. They purchased land, a mini-farm next to his WWII buddy, Joe. In the process of tossing out old stuff and digging through boxes, Bill came upon a leather bound key locked diary. The leather was old and parched and the lock was broken. Bill called to Sarah to come and see.

Sarah brushed off the dust and was amazed to find that the writing on the cover said, "This is the diary of Bill Anderson" There was also a date that went from 1861 to 1865. The penmanship inside the book was still clear and legible even though the pages were worn and fragile. So Bill and Sarah sat down to read what his great grandpa wrote. The entries were not by date or sequence. It still was like reading the script of a movie. Sarah began reading.

"My dear Susan. I decided to keep a brief record of the

events that I am currently involved in here in the Virginia countryside. The inhabitants do not welcome our Northern army and rebels that hide in farmhand clothes constantly attack us.

We have the military advantage but still the confederate army is still a formidable foe. I have given instructions to my superiors to get this diary to you in the event of my untimely death.

However, I do pray every day and some times more than once for God's protective grace and that this conflict would soon be over.

July, 1861... The Battle of Manassas

I fought along side some of the bravest men I have ever known. We charged the rebels and ended up fighting hand to hand in a violent struggle for life and victory. Many men fell on the battlefield. Some were from the North and others from the south.

Today I killed three rebels. One looked to be about 14 years old. I was deeply saddened that they died but it's war and folks die in wars. I hope that God will forgive me.

The Days After The Battle--I survived *Manassas* but was assigned to a burial detail with 25 other soldiers. We made sure those who died were honored in their sacrifice. I kept a record of names and personal belongings for my superior, Captain Clarke.

Them Johnny Rebs beat us good. But it ain't over yet. It's just one battle.

Now I spend much of my time in camp enduring long hours of boredom, followed by daily drills and picket and guard duty. I thought this was going to be an adventure. Instead, it's a war of nerves as we all wait for the next conflict.

The Battle of Shiloh
The Battle of Pittsburg Landing

God saved my life today. I was on the battlefield. It was dark with canons blasting everywhere. The sound came to charge so we did but the trumpet that sounded was not ours. It was those darn rebels that sounded the charge. So both armies charged at each other in the middle of the night. It was a confused mess.

I ran and ran and suddenly fell from a canon blast. It should have blown my legs clean off but it didn't. I was shaken but untouched by the blast. I looked up towards the moonlight as if to say, "Thank You" to God but instead saw a mysterious stranger. He was smiling at me.

I started to get up and looked away to get my footing. When I looked back, he was gone. He was dressed in all white clothing and had a bearded face. I think God sent me an angel. I sure needed one.

Dear Diary…I guess I will live and not die in this forsaken place. My dream is to return to my wife and have kids and live a good life in these here United States.

Sarah concludes…there are no more entries.

Bill…wow, he also saw the Mysterious Stranger. That guy gets around.

"Be not forgetful to entertain strangers: for thereby some have entertained angels unawares."

Hebrews 13:2

You never know when or where a "Mysterious Stranger" will drop into your world unannounced. The Bible says that these "Mysterious Strangers" are ministering spirits that are doing the will of God in the earth related to His children.

If angels are real, and I am sure they are, we should know more about them. However, they are not God. Nor are they to be worshiped.

Biblical Examples of Angels In Action

The book of Hebrews calls angels "ministering spirits sent to serve those who will inherit salvation." (Hebrews 1:14)

Here are a few ways angels minister.

Provisions..."*The Lord uses His angels to physically provide for His children. It was an angel who brought Elijah bread and water while fleeing from Jezebel after his victory on Mt. Carmel.*" 1 Kings 19:5-6

Guidance... "*But while he thought on these things, behold, the angel of the LORD appeared unto him in a dream, saying, Joseph, thou son of David, fear not to take unto thee Mary thy wife: for that which is conceived in her is of the Holy Ghost. And she* *shall bring forth a son, and thou shalt call his name JESUS: for he shall save his people from their sins."* Matthew 1:20-21

Encouragement... *"And now I exhort you to be of good cheer: for there shall be no loss of any man's life among you, but of the ship. For there stood by me this night the angel of God, whose I am, and whom I serve, Saying, Fear not, Paul; thou must be brought before Caesar: and, lo, God hath given thee all them that sail with thee."* Acts 27:22-24

Protection... *"My God hath sent his angel, and hath shut the lions' mouths, that they have not hurt me."* Daniel 6:23

Rescue or Deliverance... *"And when Herod would have brought him forth, the same night Peter was sleeping between two soldiers, bound with two chains: and the keepers before the door kept the prison. And, behold, the angel of the Lord came upon him, and a light shined in the prison: and he smote Peter on the side, and raised him up, saying, arise up quickly.*

And his chains fell off from his hands. And the angel said unto him, Gird thyself, and bind on thy sandals. And so he did. And he saith unto him, Cast thy garment about thee, and follow me. And he went out, and followed him; and wist not that it was true which was done by the angel; but thought he saw a vision.

When they were past the first and the second ward, they came unto the iron gate that leads unto the city; which opened to them of his own accord: and they went out, and passed on through one street; and forthwith the angel departed from him. And when Peter was come to himself, he said, now I know of a surety, that the Lord hath sent his angel, and hath delivered me out of the hand of Herod, and from all the expectation of the people of the Jews. Acts 12:6-11

Healing... *"Then saith Jesus unto him, Get thee hence, Satan: for it is written, Thou shalt worship the Lord thy God, and him only shalt thou serve. Then the devil left him, and, behold, angels came and ministered unto him."* Matthew 4:10-11

Also in the garden, *"An angel came from heaven to strengthen him."*

During his agony as he prayed, *"his sweat was as it were great drops of blood falling down upon the ground".* **Luke 22:44**

It is a good thing to know that God's ministering spirits are active in the earth. Much of what they do goes un-noticed except by those that have an encounter with the mysterious Stranger. They know that God is looking out for them.

Conclusion

The teenage romance that blossomed into love only to be cut off by war still burned in Sarah's heart. Although she felt sorrow and suffered from the effects of war and tragedy, she was able to forge ahead towards whatever destiny lay ahead, knowing that God would work everything together for her good because she loved Him and was called according to His purposes. (Romans 8:28)

Life is full of Mysteries and Miracles. They come and go through our every days as a train whistling down an old railroad track. The beauty of it all is that we can rest assured that God is with us and that He is working everything, both good and bad, together for our good, so we ultimately benefit from them all. He even sends us His ministering angels to help us along the way to Glory.

Life is all about perspective. We stand or fall on how we see things. Some can laugh and others cry over the same experience. Sometimes we laugh and cry but those that live life with joy and peace, trust in God to work it all together for their good.

Hidden Biblical Truths

There are certain Biblical truths the story. They are:

1. **The Mystery …** is that God will use anything to bless His children, even an old coin from the past. If you remember, Moses had a walking stick in his hand and God used it to open the red sea and devour the magicians' snakes. What's in your hand? It could be just what God needs to bless you.

2. **The Miracle…**is that God will go to great lengths to accomplish His will, even using a squirrel to position His provision in the right place and the right time. Remember the disobedient prophet in the Old Testament? God used the donkey he was riding to speak to him in a rebuke for his disobedience.

3. **God can heal broken bodies**, broken hearts and broken dreams. Remember the blind man that received his sight when Jesus touched him? How about the woman with an issue of blood? Or maybe the lepers that were cleansed? The

Bible is full of these types of miracles. They still happen today.

4. **Time is irrelevant with God**. He will not forget or slumber. Eternity does not punch a clock and God is never too late. Remember Lazarus that was raised from the dead? How about the scripture that says *"But do not forget this one thing dear friends: With the Lord a day is like a thousand years, and a thousand years is like a day."* **2 Peter 3:8**

5. **The future does not have to be like the past.** It can be different and usually is. Therefore if any man be in Christ, he is a new creature: old things are passed way; behold, all things are become new." **2 Corinthians 5:17**

6. **God is working in the lives of His children** even when it doesn't seem like it. " *I will not leave you comfortless*: I will come to you." **John 14:18**

7. **He is always true to His word.** "So shall my word be that goes forth out of my mouth: it shall not return unto me void, but it shall accomplish that which I please, and it shall prosper in the thing whereto I sent it." **Isaiah 55:11**

"For God so loved the world, that he gave his only begotten Son, that whosoever believeth in him should not perish, but have eternal life" **John 3:16.**

"Neither is there salvation in any other: for there is none other name under heaven given among men, whereby we must be saved." **Acts 4:12**

"Who hath saved us, and called us with an holy calling, not according to our works, but according to his own purpose and grace, which was given us in Christ Jesus before the world began." **2 Timothy 1:9**

"And it shall come to pass, that whosoever shall call on the name of the Lord shall be saved." **Acts 2:21**

"For with the heart man believeth unto righteousness; and with the mouth confession is made unto salvation." **Romans 10:10**

We are not alone in this life. He is with us and His love is all around us. Just knowing Him brings us inner peace.

I guess every soul has to decide for itself as to if there is a God and if He is really that personal.

Well that's my story. My heart is full, my life is blessed and my prayers are answered…and above all, my wife loves me. I give thanks to God for making it all happen.

About The Author

John Marinelli

Rev. Marinelli is an ordained minister, He has formed and been pastor of one church in Wisconsin and was the pastor of another in Alabama. He has also been a youth minister and evangelism director over the years.

Rev. Marinelli has authored several books including: "Rhyme Time", a children's story poem book", "The Art of Writing Christian Poetry," and "Pulpit Poems." He is also the author of over 80 eBooks on various Christian subjects. They are all free downloads from his website;

John is an accomplished Christian poet. He also dabbles in songwriting and writing one act Christian plays.

He is the Vice President of Have A Heart For Companion Animals, Inc., a "No Kill" animal welfare organization. He volunteers his time promoting fundraising events.

John is the Vice President in charge of marketing and fundraising events sponsored by Have A Heart For Companion Animals, Inc.

Rev. Marinelli is now retired from the sales and marketing arena after spending over 40 years in business-to-business and non-profit marketing. He enjoys writing Christian fiction stories, playing chess, singing karaoke and a retired lifestyle in sunny Florida.

For More Info or eMail Contact

johnmarinelli@embarqmail.com

Quiet Hours

In the silence of the quiet hours
In the presence of a new dawn,
I bow down upon my knees,
For bringing me life reborn

Taking off all the shackles,
Letting my spirit free.
I give all the thanks to Jesus,
For giving His love to me.

Written By Rev. Marilyn Marinelli

Ask Me Now

Hello my child.
How are you today?
I waited for your call,
And have much to say.

A word in due season,
To cause your Faith to soar.
A morsel of truth,
To quiet the lions roar.

So hear, my beloved,
Before you go on life's way,
And receive a special blessing
By what I have to say.

It's not by might or by power,
That you should gain success.
But by my Holy Spirit
That brings you life's very best.

Ask me now, my child
For all that you need.
For I bless everyone
Who's willing to believe.

Poem By John Marinelli

For The Joy Set before Him

I could have lived forever,

As a simple mortal man.

I could have called 10,000 angels,

Just to help me to stand.

But I laid down my life

Despising the shame.

For the joy set before me,

Was your life to gain.

I could have stayed in heaven,

As the supreme ruler of all things.

I could have played among the stars,

And listened for the flutter of angel's wings.

But I laid down my life,

Despising the shame.

For the joy set before me,

Was to know you by name.

I could have sent my armies,
To rid the world of sin.
I could have destroyed the Earth,
As I did way back then.
But I bore the suffering of the cross,
Despising the shame.
For the joy set before me,
Was to take away your pain.

I could have done a lot of things,
To make this world right.
Or I could have done nothing,
And ignored you plight.
But God so loved the world,
That I endured the shame.
For the joy set before me,
Was your love to gain.

Poem By John Marinelli